What The Hell Was She Up To?

Was she trying to make him insane? Because if that was the plan, she was doing fine.

Rearranging the furniture, cooking dinner, wearing a dress that made a man want to tear it from her body with his teeth. Lust roared through Dev's system like an out-of-control freight train. He'd done nothing but think about her all day and now there she stood, and he was praying she'd take a breath deep enough to have her breasts pop free of that dress.

She'd been home less than forty-eight hours and already she'd tossed his world into complete disorder.

This had *not* been his plan when he'd gone to her condo to bring her home. He was supposed to be the one setting the rules.

If he didn't know better, Devlin would swear she was deliberately trying to seduce him.

Dear Reader,

Being invited to take part in a continuity series for Silhouette Desire is always an honor. I love being able to work with other writers to create a community of shared characters.

In the Hudson continuity series, you've met some fascinating people. You've had glimpses of Hollywood and Beverly Hills and the movie industry. You've enjoyed some really great writers and the terrific stories they've come up with.

In *Seduced Into a Paper Marriage,* you'll meet my characters: Dev Hudson and his wife, Valerie Shelton Hudson. If you've been with this continuity since the beginning, you've already met Dev and Val in the snippets of scenes included at the backs of books two through five. I hope you've been intrigued.

Now, in the conclusion of the series, you'll see just how Dev and Val work out their problems and find their way to a happy ending.

I really do hope you've enjoyed your time with the Hudson family as much as we, the authors, enjoyed telling their stories!

Please visit my Web site at www.maureenchild.com or write to me at P.O. Box 1883, Westminster, CA 92684-1883.

Happy reading!

Maureen

MAUREEN CHILD

SEDUCED INTO A PAPER MARRIAGE

Silhouette® Desire

Published by Silhouette Books

America's Publisher of Contemporary Romance

Special thanks and acknowledgment to
Maureen Child for her contribution
to The Hudsons of Beverly Hills miniseries.

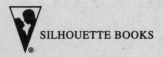

SILHOUETTE BOOKS

Recycling programs
for this product may
not exist in your area.

ISBN-13: 978-0-373-76946-9

SEDUCED INTO A PAPER MARRIAGE

Copyright © 2009 by Harlequin Books S.A.

Visit Silhouette Books at www.eHarlequin.com

Printed in U.S.A.

Books by Maureen Child

Silhouette Desire

†*Scorned by the Boss* #1816
†*Seduced by the Rich Man* #1820
†*Captured by the Billionaire* #1826
††*Bargaining for King's Baby* #1857
††*Marrying for King's Millions* #1862
††*Falling for King's Fortune* #1868
High-Society Secret Pregnancy #1879
Baby Bonanza #1893
An Officer and a Millionaire #1915
Seduced Into a Paper Marriage #1946

Silhouette Nocturne

‡*Eternally* #4
‡*Nevermore* #10
‡*Vanished* #57

†Reasons for Revenge
††Kings of California
‡The Guardians

MAUREEN CHILD

is a California native who loves to travel. Every chance they get, she and her husband are taking off on another research trip. An author of more than sixty books, Maureen loves a happy ending and still swears that she has the best job in the world. She lives in Southern California with her husband, two children and a golden retriever with delusions of grandeur. Visit her Web site at www.maureenchild.com.

To my niece, Maegan Carberry,
for always having the strength of spirit
to go her own way and fight for what she believes in.
I love you.

One

Another high-pitched squeal from the outer office went through Devlin Hudson's brain like an ice pick.

That made the fourth secretary this morning to receive either a vase full of flowers, a stuffed animal of some kind or a huge box of candy.

"Valentine's Day should be abolished," he muttered.

"That's the spirit, Boss."

He shot a quick look at his assistant, Megan Carey. The fifty-something blonde shook her head at him as if he were a personal disappointment.

"No comments from you, thanks." He knew from long experience that it was best to cut Megan off at the pass rather than let her start in on whatever was bugging her.

"I'm not saying a thing."

"That'd be a first," he said, just under his breath.

Dev was under no misapprehension. He might be the oldest sibling in the Hudson family. Might hold a position of power in the Hudson Pictures dynasty. Might even have a glare that could freeze agents and actors in their tracks. But Megan Carey ran his office— and therefore his world—and assumed the right to speak her mind no matter what he thought of the idea.

"But," she said, just to prove his thoughts right on target, "Valentine's Day is tomorrow."

"Good God." He nearly groaned. "We've got another full day of deliveries to live through."

"Man," Megan murmured, "the Romance Fairy never paid you a single visit, did she?"

"Don't you have work to do?" he countered, fixing her with a cold stare he usually reserved for over-budget directors.

"Trust me," she said with a dramatic sigh, "talking to you about this *is* work."

He almost smiled. Almost. "Fine. Say it so I can get on with my day."

"Okay, I will."

As if anything could have stopped her.

She laid a stack of phone messages on his desk, then planted both hands on her substantial hips. "Like I was saying. Valentine's Day is tomorrow. A wise man would see this as an opportunity to send his wife some flowers. Or candy. Or both."

Dev snatched up the while-you-were-gone messages and fixed his gaze on them as if she weren't there. As if ignoring her would make her go away. It didn't work.

"I'm thinking," she continued, "that any wife

would be happy to hear from her husband on such a special day—"

"Valerie and I are separated, Megan," he reminded her tightly. Dev didn't want to talk about his marriage, his wife or the fact that she'd walked out on him. On *him*.

But now that Megan had brought it up, his brain picked up the torch and ran with it.

Dev still could hardly believe that his wife had left him. For God's sake, *why?* They'd gotten along all right. She'd had an open account at every store on Rodeo Drive and the free time to do all the shopping she wanted. They had lived in his suite at the family mansion, so she hadn't even had to concern herself with dealing with house-keepers. All she'd had to do was live with him.

Which, apparently, hadn't been enough of a draw to keep her there.

So now, he was a husband whose wife lived in an upscale condo in Beverly Hills, who was often photographed shopping or doing lunch at some trendy restaurant in town and who might, for all Dev knew, be *dating*.

His fist tightened around the stack of messages until the papers folded in on themselves like a broken accordion. Dating—his *wife*—unacceptable, he told himself even as he realized there wasn't a damn thing he could do about it.

"That's right boss," Megan said, approval ringing in her tone. "You're *separated,* not divorced."

"Megan," he ground out, "if you value your job, you'll drop this. Now."

She snorted. "Oh, please. You couldn't run this place without me, and we both know it."

A deep voice spoke up from the doorway. "If he fires you, Megan, I'll hire you at twice the salary."

Dev looked at his brother Max. "Hell, I'll pay you to take her."

Megan frowned at both of them. "I should quit. Just to prove to you how indispensable I am around here. But I won't, because I'm just too good a person to watch this place fold without me."

She left with her nose in the air and a final scowl for both of them as she turned to close the door behind her.

Dev leaned back in his black-leather chair. "Why don't I fire her?"

Max strolled across the huge office and took the chair opposite his brother. "Because," he said as he sat down and got comfortable, "she's been here thirty years, has known us both since we were kids and would probably kill us both if we *tried* to get rid of her."

"Good point." Dev shook his head and let his gaze slide around the room. He barely noticed the framed movie posters hanging on his walls, the conference table, the wet bar, the functional yet comfortable furniture or even the view of the back lot of Hudson Pictures' studios that lay outside the wide windows.

This was his world. This was where he did the work that made him happy.

So why the *hell* wasn't he happy?

"What was she on you about now?"

Dev shot Max a quick look. "She thinks I should send Val flowers for Valentine's Day."

"Not a bad idea," his brother mused, steepling his fingers together. "I just sent Dana sterling roses and a giant box of Godiva. Why shouldn't you send some-thing to Val?"

"Are you insane?" Dev shot to his feet and stalked the perimeter of the room. "You want to buy into this Valentine thing for your fiancée, fine. But Val walked out on me, remember?"

"Not really surprising, was it?"

"What's that supposed to mean?"

"Well, come on, Dev. She was nuts about you and you hardly noticed she was there."

He stopped dead, swiveled his head to glare at his younger brother and said, "My marriage is none of your business."

Max only shrugged. "I'm only saying that if you put as much effort into keeping your wife happy as you did with placating whiny directors, you wouldn't be alone right now."

"Thanks very much, Mr. Newly In Love and Newly Annoying."

Max smiled. "I admit it. I'm grateful to have found Dana. After I lost Karen…"

Dev winced. He hadn't meant to bring up his brother's late wife or the misery he'd lived through for so long. "Look, I'm glad you're happy. But that doesn't mean everybody else is looking for what you have."

"You should."

"Damn it, Max, did you come here to lecture me on my love life? What are you, some love guru now?"

"Hardly!" Max laughed shortly. "But since Megan was already on your ass, thought I'd join in."

"Thanks so much. But no thanks. Love is for morons."

For the last year, the entire Hudson family had been

tumbling into love and marriage and happily ever afters. And they were damned irritating on the subject—all of them.

Well, Dev wasn't convinced. They were in the movie business. Hudson Pictures *sold* happy endings to the public. That didn't mean that Dev believed in them.

"Says every man who doesn't have a woman around on Valentine's Day." Max shook his head and grinned.

Dev shot Max a hard look that didn't do a thing toward dimming his brother's self-satisfied smile. "I can't believe even you're buying into this. Valentine's Day? You're serious? Every male in the world knows that the holiday was invented by card manufacturers and candymakers. It's a woman's holiday, little brother. Not a man's."

"A little candy, a few flowers and some wine and there's a great evening for both of you. Of course," Max mused, "you wouldn't know anything about that, would you? Oh, no. You're the guy who let his wife leave him on Christmas Eve. Mr. Romance."

"You know something? You're far less amusing now that you're in love."

"Funny," Max mused. "Your marriage didn't change your personality at all."

No, it hadn't. But then, Dev told himself, he hadn't gone into his marriage claiming to be "in love," either. He'd married Valerie because he'd needed a wife and she had fit the requirements perfectly. She had good connections —press, media, corporate—and she looked lovely on his arm.

At least she *had,* until she left him. Not that he missed her or anything. He was fine with Val being gone. Completely fine.

"Exactly my point," he said firmly. "I'm the same man I was when I got married."

"And that's a damn shame," Max told him.

Frowning, Dev walked to the wide bank of windows and stared out the glass. There were acres of land out there, all belonging to Hudson Pictures. There was the back lot, where dozens of different sets stood, just waiting for camera crews to arrive and bring them to life again. There were actors and extras, stagehands and electricians. The studio back lot was a small city and he was its mayor.

But instead of seeing his domain, nestled deep in the heart of Burbank, Dev's mind furnished a mental view of Beverly Hills. Where Valerie now lived in a condo that he'd never seen the inside of.

Glancing back at his brother, Dev kept his voice low and demanded, "What's that supposed to mean?"

"It means, Dev, that you could use a little lightening up."

Max turned his chair so that he was facing Dev. "Val was your shot at actually having a real life and you let her waltz right out the door."

Gritting his teeth, he shifted his gaze back to the city view. He didn't want to talk about his marriage. Not with Max. Not with anyone.

The irritation that had spiked inside him the night Val left—Christmas Eve, no less—was still with him. He was Devlin Hudson. Nobody walked out on him. At least no one ever *had* until Val. And dealing with the very public aftermath of his marriage's collapse had left Dev with a bitter taste in his mouth and his hackles continually on the rise.

Every newspaper and gossip rag in the city had speculated as to the reason for Val leaving him. There'd been paparazzi after the two of them for weeks and though he hated to admit it, even to himself, Dev had sunk so low as to checking out the tabloids just to catch any news of what his wife was up to.

He turned abruptly, walked back to his desk and sat down again. Only when he had the breadth of the desk between him and his brother did he say, "Did it ever occur to you that I was the one who wanted the separation?"

"Nope." Max shook his head, leaned back in his chair and stretched out his legs, crossing his feet at the ankle. He looked as relaxed as a man could get in an eight-hundred-dollar suit. "See, Dev, that's not your style. Once you make a deal, you stick to it. So, no, you wouldn't have asked her to go. The only thing I can't figure out is why you *allowed* her to leave."

"Allow?" Now Dev laughed and folded his hands together atop his abdomen. "You do a lot of 'allowing' in your relationship, do you? I think Dana would disagree."

For the first time, Max frowned, clearly trying to imagine using the word "allow" and Dana in the same sentence, then looked slightly less relaxed. "Touché. Okay, maybe *allow* was the wrong word. But what the hell were you thinking letting her leave you? It was clear to everybody in the family that Val was nuts about you."

She had been, Dev remembered as Max and the office drifted away on a tide of memories. Val had always been so damn eager for time with him. Her eyes shining, smile bright. She'd gone into a relationship with him with anticipation and enthusiasm. He'd taken it for granted, of course. Why wouldn't he? He'd known she loved him. That was only one of the reasons he'd been so sure that marrying her was the right move. How could he go wrong if his wife loved him?

More memories crowded his mind. Valerie, smiling at him. Val in France on the set of the movie, *Honor.* Val in their bed, giving him a wan smile after their disastrous wedding night. Damn it. Devlin actually squirmed in his chair at that memory.

But in his defense, he hadn't expected her to be a virgin. Hadn't thought for a minute that she'd be nervous, wound so tight every nerve was a live wire and a little toasted to boot.

Not his proudest moment, he admitted silently. He had wanted her badly and hadn't bothered with seduction. Sex that night had been a misery, and because of that, every attempt at lovemaking after that had been just as bad. Memories were a hard thing to defeat, and Dev hadn't been able to get past his own regrets and her burgeoning fears to make sex anything more than a disaster.

Pushing his dark thoughts aside, he focused on Max and said clearly, "It's none of the family's business."

"This is about Mom and Dad, isn't it? About their marriage."

Devlin speared a hard look at his brother. Since finding out that his own mother had cheated in her marriage to Dev's father, Devlin hadn't had a lot of faith in the sanctity of matrimony. Sure, it had colored his outlook a little. Why wouldn't it? The two people he'd always considered close to perfect had turned out to have feet of clay.

"Leave them out of this."

"Why? You're not." Max sighed. "You won't talk to Dad about this, won't hear Mom out and you're like the damn ice man around the rest of us."

"I've been working," Dev announced on a growl of irritation. "Maybe you haven't noticed but we've got a few films in postproduction, not to mention that little Academy Award nomination...."

"This isn't about work, Dev. This is about you. Your life. All you had to do was try, man." Max frowned at him. "Val loved you, and you blew it."

Regret stabbed at him again and Devlin didn't like the feel of it. He wasn't a man to look backward. He never had been one to think over past mistakes and try to figure out where he'd gone wrong. The past was past and there wasn't a damn thing you could do to change it.

Deliberately, Dev stood up and looked down at his brother. "I didn't blow a damn thing. And I should think you'd be better off spending time on your own love life instead of worrying about me and my wife."

"You don't have a wife, Dev," Max reminded him.

Funny, he'd said the same thing to Megan just awhile ago, but now, hearing Max say those words was enough to jumpstart a ball of fury in the pit of his stomach. But Megan was right. He *did* have a wife. He just didn't have her with him. Well, fine, he couldn't fix the past. But he could for damn sure do something about the future.

"Yeah, I do," he countered, realizing that he was sick

to death of fielding reporters' questions, dodging photographers and putting up with his own family's incessant prodding about Val. It was time he straightened this mess out.

After all, why the hell was *he* dealing with all of this?

He wasn't the one who'd walked out on their marriage. He wasn't the one who'd wanted to wander around an empty suite of rooms and listen to the silence. She'd put them through all of this, and he was damned tired of living with the situation she'd created.

"That'll be news to Val," Max said, pushing himself out of his chair.

"You let me worry about Val." The more he thought about this, the better he felt. Riding a surge of righteous anger, Dev stalked across the room, threw open the closet door and grabbed his suit jacket off a hanger.

"Where're you going?" Max demanded.

"I'm going to have a long talk with my wife," Dev said. And as the thought of seeing her again fixated in his mind, he realized just how much he'd missed her, damn it. "Time I reminded Val that we're still married."

"You think it's going to be that easy?"

Dev looked at his younger brother. For the past few days, he'd been surrounded by googly-eyed secretaries, assistants and family members. It seemed every time he turned around there was a box of candy or a bouquet of flowers being delivered to the office.

The hearts and flowers of Valentine's Day had only served to remind him over the past few days just how alone he really was. The emptiness he faced when he went home nagged at him. Watching his brothers and sister revel in their own romances was bothering him on a level he wouldn't have thought possible before now.

Why that was, he didn't really want to think about. After all, he'd been alone most of his life. By choice.

And maybe that was the real motivator here. He hadn't chosen to be alone. He'd been forced into it by a decision Valerie had made all by herself. Well, she'd had her say. She'd walked out. Gotten all the "space" anyone could possibly want. But that was over. It was time she came home. Lived up to the marriage vows they'd made. Nobody had said anything about *until you feel like leaving.* No. It had been *until death do you part.* When Dev took an oath, he kept it. He expected no less from his wife.

And it was past time he told her that.

Smiling grimly at Max, he said, "Easy or not, it's going to be done."

Valerie Shelton Hudson had her own condo overlooking the hills and trees and mansions of Beverly Hills. It was plush, luxurious, tastefully decorated and so damned empty she wanted to scream just to hear some noise.

She rarely turned on the television or the radio, though—she didn't want to hear anything about Hudson Pictures or the upcoming Academy Awards. Every time she heard Devlin's name, her heart ached and the loneliness that had become such a part of her threatened to swallow her whole.

So instead of thinking about what she'd lost, she'd devoted herself to as little thinking as possible. She went to lunch with her friends, volunteered at her favorite charities, did some shopping and tried to ignore the paparazzi who tended to leap out at her, cameras clicking, every time she left her home.

She managed to fill her days, but her nights were empty, quiet, lonely. She wasn't interested in dating and couldn't bring herself to hit any of the trendy night-spots with her friends. So nights were long and days were crowded and still she found time to miss her husband. Miss the very man who had ignored her so completely that her only option had been to leave him.

"This is not the way I want to live," she muttered and stepped out onto the secluded, private patio off her living room.

A jumble of plants greeted her. There were ferns in hanging pots, flowers spilling out of ceramic tubs, neatly trimmed bushes and even a small lemon tree in the corner. There was a chrome-and-tile table and four decorative café chairs pulled up to it. There was also a patio swing boasting a bright red and yellow awning and it was to that spot she headed. Curled up on the swing, she could listen to the distant hum of traffic fifteen stories below her and know that in at least *this* place, she had privacy.

A place to think. Unfortunately, the minute she started thinking, her thoughts turned to Devlin. Scowling to herself, she pushed aside the image of him that raced into her mind: the stunned look on his face when she'd told him she was leaving. She hated re-membering that she had turned tail and run away. She hated that she hadn't dug her heels in and fought for the marriage she'd wanted.

Oh, at first, she'd blamed Devlin for the inglorious

end to their marriage. But now, she was forced to admit that there was enough blame to go around for both of them. She hadn't ever spoken up for herself. Hadn't made him *see* her. Instead, she'd waited quietly—like a big idiot—for him to feel the same sparks she had the moment she'd met him.

She picked up a throw pillow, hugged it to her chest and leaned her head against the back of the swing. Closing her eyes, she allowed Dev's image to rise up in her mind again and in an instant everything in her body went into a slow burn.

God, she wished she could do it all over again. She'd do so many things differently.

"First off, I wouldn't be so damned accommodating," she muttered, eyes still closed as she studied the mental image of Dev. "I'd speak up for myself. Spend less time trying to be the perfect little wife and more time being myself." She choked on that last sentence.

Perfect little wife.

"Good God, no wonder he was bored. Could anything be more horrifying?" Groaning, she hugged that pillow tighter to her midsection and felt frustration bubbling up inside her. It was a familiar feeling these days.

"Ms. Hudson?"

Valerie sighed at her housekeeper's interruption, but didn't lift her head or open her eyes. "Yes, Teresa?"

"There's someone to see you," the other woman said quietly, almost apologetically. "I told him you didn't want to be disturbed, but—"

"I wouldn't take no for an answer."

Valerie's head shot up, her eyes flew open and her gaze locked on the one person she'd never expected to see again.

Her husband.

Two

"Surprised?" Dev walked past the housekeeper, strolled out onto the patio and, with his hands in the pockets of his slacks, looked completely at ease.

"Yeah, I'm surprised." She stared at him as if he were an apparition and Dev couldn't tell if that meant she was happy to see him or not.

"I need to talk to you." Dev's gaze slipped from her to the housekeeper and back again.

Val took a deep breath, braced herself and glanced at the woman waiting in the doorway. "It's all right, Teresa. I'll be fine."

The older woman didn't look convinced. As she turned to go, she said plainly, "If you need me, Ms. Hudson, just call."

When she was gone, Dev actually laughed. "Your own private dragon?"

"I don't need a dragon at the gates, Dev. I can take care of myself."

One dark eyebrow rose as he watched her, then slowly, he nodded. "I expect you could."

"So, we're alone now. Why don't you tell me what this is about?"

She didn't sound exactly welcoming, but it didn't really matter. He'd come on a mission, damn it, and he was going to see it through. He'd thought about this all the way over here and he knew precisely the tack he was going to take with Val. He'd simply point out to her that this separation was ridiculous. They were married. They should be together. And, he'd remind her that the Oscars were fast approaching and that he wanted the Hudson family to show a united front.

All reasonable.

He was sure he'd convince her.

"Why are you here?"

Surprised himself now, Dev looked at her and watched as she tossed the throw pillow to one side and stood up. When she faced him, her chin was raised and her eyes were staring directly into his. All right, that was different. The Val he knew—the one he'd expected to find—was nowhere to be seen. She would have stayed curled up on the swing, hidden behind a pillow and keeping her gaze averted.

Still, a little backbone was a good thing.

"I've come to bring you home."

"I am home," she countered and walked to the table and chairs. She pulled out one of the tiny, more decorative than useful seats and sat down, staring up at him.

"I meant," he said, keeping his voice even, "our home. The family mansion."

"I don't live there anymore," she told him.

A flicker of temper flashed inside him, but he quickly tamped it down. He'd been in enough negotiations to know that an even keel was necessary to accomplish your goals. Pulling out the chair closest to him, Dev sat down beside her, braced his elbows on his knees and looked into her eyes.

"Yeah, you left. I remember."

"Then why—"

He held up one hand to cut her off. "It's been a couple of months now, Val. I think you've made your point."

"My point?" Her big eyes went even wider.

"You wanted to let me know you were unhappy. I get that. And I'm willing to talk this out and do whatever's necessary to get you back where you belong."

There was a long pause while she considered the speech he'd worked out on the drive to her house. He'd been logical, thoughtful and thorough. No one could ask for more.

"Why?"

He blinked at her. "What?"

"Not what," she countered. "Why. Why do you want me back?"

"You're my wife."

She blew out a breath before saying, "Okay then, why now? Why not a month ago? Why not a month from now? Why are you here today, Dev?"

He sat up, leaned one arm on the table and felt the cool, knobby glass beneath his hand. He hadn't expected questions. The Val he was used to would have simply agreed and gone along with his plan. *That* Val would have made this much easier.

Thinking fast, he told her, "Tomorrow's Valentine's Day."

"So?"

He should have brought flowers. Or candy. Or as Megan had suggested, *both*. Since he hadn't, he dropped the reference to the most romantic day on the calendar and went in another direction.

"It made me realize how much time has gone by," he said. Reasonable again. "The Academy Awards will be here soon, and I think it's important for the Hudson family to be together when we win for Best Picture."

"I see."

Not a flicker of emotion on her face. Dev couldn't tell what she was thinking and that bothered him more than he wanted to admit. Something else was bothering him as well, though. Something more disconcerting than trying to discover who this new, mysterious Val was.

One look at her and his body had gone tight and hard and eager. Damn it. Even remembering how disastrous the sex had been between them, he couldn't deny that he still wanted her. Badly enough that simply sitting, at the moment, was uncomfortable.

So he stood up. He took two steps, stopped, then whirled around to face her. "Look, my point is, we're married. We both knew what we were doing when we went into this marriage. We agreed when we first got together that there would be no divorce."

They'd both seen firsthand how out of control the cycle of marriage and divorce could get—especially in this town. And neither of them had wanted any part of that.

"True," she agreed.

"Good," he said, smiling now. His point made, he could afford to be magnanimous. "So you'll come home."

She stood up slowly, unfolding herself from the chair with a fluid sort of grace that gave her a suppleness that fed the flames already crouched inside Dev. He bit back a groan as she faced him.

"*If* I come home," she said, capturing his attention immediately, "there are a couple of conditions."

"Excuse me?" He hadn't expected *this*.

Valerie really enjoyed the expression of stunned disbelief on his face. Oh God, why hadn't she been more herself from the beginning? If she'd only shown him the real Valerie, so much heartache and misery could have been avoided. On both sides.

Well, she told herself, feeling a rush of excitement build within, she was getting a second chance. Devlin still didn't love her, she knew that. But he wanted her back. Had come to her home to get her to return to him. That was a huge plus for her side. And if he was willing to go that far, then surely he'd go a little further.

"If we do this," she said, meeting and holding his gaze, "then we do it differently this time."

"What do you mean, differently?" His expression was guarded now.

"I mean, I want a *real* marriage, Dev. Not the polite, distant merger we had before."

"Meaning?"

His eyes narrowed on her, but Val stood her ground. She wasn't the spineless, shy little Stepford Wife he thought her to be. She was a woman with her own mind and enough courage to face down the man she loved and tell him that she'd rather leave than have only half of him. If she'd had the strength to walk out on him, then she had the strength to fight for him.

"I want you to spend time with me. I want a partnership."

"Valerie—"

"Oh, no. Don't take that oh-so-patient tone with me, either, Dev," she said, cutting him off neatly before he could give her the figurative pat on the head he so clearly wanted to do.

His features went tight and hard, but she wasn't going to be dissuaded from saying exactly what she thought. Not this time. If they were going to try again, then Val wanted the brass ring this time around.

"You always use that specific tone of voice when you want to politely tell me to back off."

"No, I don't—"

"You did, too, but not anymore, okay?" She walked in closer, which wasn't easy because her knees were a little wobbly and the slow burn she'd felt the moment he walked onto her patio had become an inferno, spreading through her veins.

"Is that right?"

"Yep." She smiled up at him and watched, pleased, as his eyes flashed. "I'm your wife, Dev. And if we're going to do this marriage right, then I want more of your attention. There's something else, too. I know we didn't start off right, but I want you in my bed."

He nodded. "Good—"

"I want children."

"Children?"

"Doesn't have to be today," she amended when he got that deer-in-the-headlights look in his eyes. "But someday soon. I want a family, Dev. And for this to work, that means that I'll need you to devote to me at least a *quarter* of the energies you show to Hudson Pictures."

"That's quite the list of conditions."

"It is," she said and folded her arms across her chest to hide the nerves beginning to shake through her. She'd done the right thing, speaking up, letting him know she wouldn't go back to being his own private doormat. But now that she'd made her play and placed her bet, she was forced to wait to see if Dev was willing to start their marriage over again—the right way.

His gaze fixed on her, Dev scraped one hand across his jaw. Seconds ticked past and the nerves quaking inside her began to rattle like dice in a cup. Though Dev looked irritated, he, as always, had a tight grip on that control of his. He never let his emotions rule him.

That legendary control of his was the first thing Valerie had to break through. If she could just get him to open up, to let himself go, they might just stand a chance of making this work.

And the minute that thought flashed through her mind, she knew exactly what she was going to have to do to accomplish it. She would have to use sex to break down the walls he'd built up around himself. She knew it instinctively. Despite the fact that their lovemaking so far had been awkward and restrained, she knew that he wanted her as badly as she did him. All she had to do was seduce him into losing his self-control.

Sure, she told herself wryly, no problem.

"Say I agree…"

She stopped thinking and held her breath.

"What's to stop you from walking out again the next time you feel…unappreciated?"

"My word," she said, meeting that cold, hard gaze of his steadily. It was a fair question and he had no way of knowing that she'd been kicking herself silly ever since she'd left him. No, if she went back to him, it was for good. No more running. No more backing off. This time she was in it to win her husband or die trying.

"I give you my word," she said, "that if we start over, I won't leave unless you *want* me to."

"That won't happen," he said softly, his gaze dropping now to sweep over her body like a caress. She felt heat racing across her skin and her body nearly hummed with a sense of anticipation.

"Then we have nothing to worry about, do we?" God, was she doing the right thing? Yes, she answered that question immediately. She still loved Dev. She wanted a marriage with him. And if she could just make him see what they could have together, it would all be worth it.

"Well, then," he said, stepping in closer, cupping her shoulders with his big, warm hands, "looks like we have a deal, Mrs. Hudson."

"Looks like we do, Mr. Hudson," she said and silently congratulated herself on speaking at all. Her throat was tight and the heat rushing through her felt like magma, thick in her veins.

He was wearing that cologne she loved on him, with the mingled scents of spice and citrus. This close to her husband, Val could hardly breathe and she wondered just how she'd managed to live through the last couple of months without seeing him.

Touching him.

As he was now touching her. His hands moved up and down her arms, creating a friction on her bare skin that felt almost electrical with the buzz it created. She took a breath, held it for a second, then let it go as she stared up into his startlingly blue eyes.

"You surprised me today, Val," he said, his voice a hush of sound she had to strain to hear. "You were always so quiet. So…"

She frowned a bit. "Accommodating?"

He smiled. "Maybe."

"Disappointed?" she asked as his hands swept up her arms to cup her face.

"What do you think?" He lowered his head and kissed her.

His mouth claimed hers, his tongue parted her lips and swept inside her warmth, stealing away what breath she had left. She melted into the hard, broad wall of his chest and gave herself up to incredible sensations as they crested and peaked one after another inside her.

His lips, his tongue, made love to her mouth as he shifted his hands to slide down her spine to the curve of her behind. Then he held her, pressed her tightly to the hard, thickness of his body until she knew exactly just how much he wanted her.

The kiss went on and on and Val lost all track of time. Nothing else mattered. Nothing else was as important as this moment, here with him, when her life was starting over, when she felt the first stirrings of hope that one day she would have the marriage and the *man* she'd always dreamed of.

Then he broke the kiss, raised his head and looked down at her through dark, desire-filled eyes. "Let's get your stuff and go home."

"Right."

He took her hand and led her back into the condo and Val could only think that maybe the seduction of Devlin Hudson wasn't going to be as difficult as she'd thought.

Three

Moving her things to the mansion wasn't as difficult as Val would have imagined. Dev had a way of getting things done when it was something he wanted.

Almost before she knew it, her bags were packed, Teresa was given an enormous severance package and Val was back in Dev's suite of rooms at the Hudson family estate.

As she unpacked, she couldn't help remembering the last time she'd been there: the afternoon of Christmas Eve when she'd faced Dev and told him she was leaving him. She could still remember the look of stunned disbelief on his face as he'd heard her out. And she'd known then that he'd been more shocked by someone actually defying him than he had been by her leaving.

Devlin Hudson never lost. At anything.

And as if to prove that out, here she was, back again.

"But I'm not the same Val," she reassured herself. "Things will be different this time. I'm not going to be the convenient wife again. No more appearing when he wants me and disappearing when he doesn't. I'm here and he's just going to have to learn to live with it."

Of course, she'd been back at the mansion for an hour and so far, nothing had changed. Dev had dropped her off and gone back to work to "clear up a few things."

A bad start to their fresh beginning? she wondered. But as soon as that thought slid through her mind, she banished it. She wasn't going to start off resenting him. Valerie already knew that it would take her some time to win Dev's affections. Breaking down a wall he'd spent his entire life building wasn't going to be done overnight.

When her last blouse had been hung and the last sweater tucked away, she turned to look around Dev's— *their*—bedroom. She smiled to herself. No more of this his-and-hers bedroom stuff anymore, either. When they first got married, Dev had insisted that she choose one of the extra rooms in the suite as her own sanctuary. But as things between them had become more and more strained, she'd found herself, more often than not, retreating to the room that had become more of a hideout than sanctuary.

This time, she wasn't going to give herself a chance to hide away and lick her wounds. She wasn't going to give either one of them a chance to go back to the awkward behavior that had so ruined their sex life—and their marriage—before. Nope. If they were going to be married, then she was going to be right here.

In his bed.

Where he couldn't ignore her.

She wanted to share his bed every night and wake up beside him every morning. She wanted to become such a part of his life that he couldn't imagine a world without her in it. And this bed would be her battle-ground.

Okay, yes, she was a little nervous. But she'd spent the last several weeks thinking of everything that had gone wrong between her and Dev. Telling herself what she could have done differently.

Now was her chance.

She looked at the extra-wide, king-size mattress covered by a black duvet and mounded with pillows. Soft, late afternoon light crept through the opened drapes and lay across the bed as if in invitation. Thank-fully, she thought, their wedding night had not been spent in this bed, so there were no lingering, uncomfort-able memories associated with it. This was a new start and, as she looked at the bed, Val's mind filled with erotic images, all flashing through her brain in a dizzying sort of slide show.

Dev looming over her. Dev taking her in the shower. His hands stroking her skin even as she reached to touch him everywhere. Her heart pounded and her blood ran suddenly thick in her veins.

"Whoa." She swallowed hard and slapped one hand to her abdomen in a futile attempt to still the swarms of butterflies racing around inside. Then she shook her head at her own uneasiness. "You're not the same wimpy little virgin you were before, Val. You know you want him—so go get him already."

Monologue pep talks.

"Great. Not only am I talking to myself, I'm cheering myself up. Can't be a good sign."

Blowing out a breath, she left the bedroom, walked down a short hall and into the massive family room/den.

A stone fireplace crouched against one wall and its mantel was filled with framed family photos. On the beige walls, paintings by artists both famous and unknown were hung side by side. Brown leather couches and chairs were drawn up in conversational groups and heavy oak tables held stacks of books and scripts along with shaded Tiffany lamps. There was a wet bar in one corner and a 52-inch plasma TV on the far wall.

The room was beautiful, but it was also completely male. When she'd lived here before, she'd been too timid to try to put her stamp on Dev's place, so instead she'd left herself to feel like a temporary roommate in his home.

"Well, that ship has sailed," she promised the empty room, already planning some shopping and redecorating excursions.

Being here was both familiar and strange all at the same time. In the months they lived there together, Valerie had tried to fit into Dev's life rather than convincing him to build a new life for both of them. She'd put her own wants and desires aside, foolishly believing that if she was everything he needed, he would want her.

Now she knew that he could never really want *her* if he never knew who she actually was.

So, until her marriage was on solid ground and she could talk him into buying their own home, then she would have to find a way to make this place her home, as well as his. It might not be easy living here, but she could do it.

She laughed suddenly, appalled at her own thoughts. "Such a hardship, Val. Being *forced* to live in an entire wing of a palatial mansion in Beverly Hills. You poor baby."

Stupid to feel sorry for yourself while standing in what was practically a castle. But until she'd carved out a slice of this place for herself, she was just going to feel unsettled.

Smiling a little wistfully, she walked across the big area to the second-story balcony that overlooked the sweep of lawn to the side of the house. She opened the French doors, stepped onto the stone patio and lifted her face to the breeze sighing through the ancient trees surrounding the estate.

When she opened her eyes again, she noticed it was close to sunset. Already, brilliant shades of crimson and violet were staining the sky. Soon, Dev would be coming home. Nerves she was all too familiar with fluttered to life again in the pit of her stomach.

But this time, she deliberately fought them down. She wouldn't let her own sense of uneasiness ruin this before it had even begun. She was a wife who wanted her husband. A wife who had finally decided to steer her marriage down the path she wanted it to take. So, nerves or not, she was going through with her plan.

And, she thought firmly as she headed back inside, when he walked in the door, Devlin was going to have quite the surprise waiting for him.

Dev would have agreed to any of Val's terms—in theory. He wanted his wife back where she belonged. And once she was settled in the mansion again, she'd forget about her "conditions." Their marriage would return to the way it had been. With, he thought, remembering that kiss on her patio, one exception.

She wanted him in her bed? He wanted the same damn thing. They'd been too caught up in the disaster that had been their wedding night to ever overcome it. But it was past time they let that miserable night go.

He wanted his wife, damn it. As that thought registered, he admitted silently that he actually wanted her more than he'd ever expected to. Just looking at her this afternoon had fired every ounce of need and hunger locked inside him. And kissing her had pushed him closer to the edge than he had been in far too long.

Dev prided himself on his control. He kept a tight rein on all of his emotions at all times. He wasn't one to be led around by his desire and he wasn't one to open himself up to feelings that could potentially turn around and bite him.

But he wasn't prepared to live the life of a guilt-ridden monk, either. Yes, their wedding night had been bad and the few times they'd made love after that, he'd held back because he could still see the misery in her eyes. That time was past, though. She wanted a fresh start and he could ensure they had it.

This time, he was prepared to give her the seduction she needed to get past the fears that were no doubt still crowding her mind.

If he'd simply done this from the beginning, she never would have left, he reminded himself. This time, he was determined to get things right.

Hence the giant bouquet of flowers and the huge box of Godiva chocolates lying on the passenger seat of his sports car. He hated like hell that he was buying into the whole Valentine's Day thing, but this was a special occasion. His wife was home where she belonged and he wanted to catch her off guard. And if the flowers and candy didn't do it for him, then the slow seduction he had planned would turn the trick.

A candlelight dinner on the patio of their suite. Soft music playing on the stereo. A dance in the moonlight. By the time he was through with her, she'd be melting into his arms.

Smiling to himself, Dev steered the car into the circular drive in front of the mansion. He'd produced enough movies with sappy love stories in them to know exactly how to set a scene for sex.

Grabbing up the flowers and candy, Dev opened the car door, got out, then slammed it behind him. Instead of going for the front door of the house, he walked around to the side to his private entrance. No point in letting the whole house see him carrying roses and candy like some lovesick puppy.

Besides, what went on between him and his wife was their business.

The outside lights were on, tossing pale shadows of white into the encroaching darkness. Wind rustled the leaves in the trees and he heard the cheerful splash of water in the nearby fountain. He glanced to the second-story patio and caught a glimpse of white linen. Good—that meant the housekeeper had seen to the setting of the table. All he'd have to do was call down to the kitchen when they were ready to eat.

He smiled to himself as he stepped inside, ignored the family living room and took the stairs to his apartment on the second floor. He was willing to bet that Valerie had been surprised as hell to discover that he'd arranged for a candlelit dinner for the two of them.

Which meant, she was already primed for seduction. The flowers and candy would be as big a surprise and probably just enough to push her over the edge.

"The secret," Dev told himself as he hit the landing and strode down the hall to his den, "is to keep her off-balance. So that she never knows what's coming next." His fist tightened around the bouquet of roses and baby's breath as he stepped into the room.

"Surprise. That's the key," he told himself.

"Welcome home, Dev."

Dev dropped the bouquet at his feet. The box of candy followed. His jaw dropped and something deep inside him lurched unsteadily.

His wife, the woman he'd been so determined to surprise, the one who'd been so shy and awkward their first night together, was draped languidly across his favorite chair, wearing nothing but a string of pearls and her wedding ring.

She smiled, lifted the pearls to her mouth and idly nibbled at the soft, white gems. Glancing at the floor, she then lifted her gaze to his and asked, "Are those for me?"

"What?" His brain was fogged.

Dev shook his head, trying to get his mind jump-started, but all the blood in his body had drained to a spot much farther south. "You—I wasn't expecting—uh…"

She smiled and leaned her head against the arm of the chair. "What's the matter, Dev? Aren't you happy to see me?"

"Yeah." Idiot, he called himself as he stepped into the room and closed the door behind him. He'd thought to surprise *her?* Hell, his mouth was dry, his heart was pounding and his body was so tight and hard he thought he just might explode if she moved the slightest bit. "I'm…surprised—" damn it "—that's all."

"Well, good." She swung her legs off the arm of the chair and stood up slowly. Her long, lean body was even better than he remembered. High, firm breasts, narrow waist and trim legs. Her skin was the color of ripe peaches and her hair was loose and wavy about her face.

She was a temptress.

He'd never seen this side of his wife and he had to say he approved.

"I think it's time we surprised each other a little, don't you?" She was walking toward him—God help him. Each step brought her a little closer and his gaze moved over her body eagerly; he was loving the way the soft lights in the room drifted over her skin.

"That was my idea, too," he admitted and remembered that he'd dropped the gifts he'd brought home for her. Bending over, he scooped them up and held them out to her as she came closer.

"They're lovely," she murmured and buried her face in the luxurious bouquet of pale lavender roses. She lifted her gaze to his. "Chocolate, too? That's so thoughtful, Dev. Thank you."

She turned to set the flowers and candy down on the nearest table and Dev's gaze dropped to the curve of her truly luscious behind. His hands itched to touch her. His body craved hers. He wanted to toss her onto the floor and bury himself inside her.

But, he warned himself, that's just the kind of thinking that had made their wedding night so grim. No finesse. Just hunger. No seduction. Just need. He wouldn't repeat that mistake. So, though it might kill him to take it slowly, he was going to do just that.

She turned back to him, smiled into his eyes and said softly, "I want you, Dev. Now."

Something in his brain exploded.

That was the only answer.

Because he heard himself say, "Thank God," just before he grabbed her and pulled her close.

Val felt the strength in his arms and gave herself up to the wonder of knowing that his desire matched her own. What a fool she'd been when she first married him. She'd come to him too nervous to allow her own need free rein and she'd cheated herself out of these swamping waves of hunger.

His mouth came down on hers; his tongue danced with hers in a tangled web of passion that stole what little breath she had left. It had taken every ounce of her nerve to meet him naked as he walked in the door, but, oh, it had been so worth it. The look on his face when he'd first seen her would stay with her forever.

Devlin Hudson didn't know it, but Val had already won the first battle for his heart.

Then her thoughts dissolved under an onslaught of sensations that threatened to drown her. He tore his mouth from hers, buried his face in the curve of her neck and nibbled at her throat, tasting the pulse point at the base. His tongue swept over her heated skin and sent shivers of anticipation rocketing through her system.

Here was the magic she'd hoped to find on their

wedding night. What he did to her dissolved all thought and erased any of the lingering traces of anxiety she might have been feeling.

Valerie moaned softly, turned her head to give him greater access and arched into him, silently urging him on. His hands slid up and down her back, defining her spine, exploring her skin, cupping her bottom with a grip both firm and gentle. His fingers held on to her, pulling her in tightly enough that she couldn't miss feeling the hard, solid length of him pressed against her.

Her core went molten and liquid, every cell tingling and alive with expectation. Her breasts rubbed against his suit jacket and linen shirt, the fine material scraping sensuously against her sensitive skin. It was good. All good. But she wanted more. Wanted to feel his flesh against hers. Feel the heat of him sliding into her.

As if he heard her silent wish, he pulled away from her and tore his jacket and shirt off, tossing them onto the floor with no more thought than she gave them. Then he was holding her again, molding her to his broad, muscular chest, and Val sighed with contentment.

God, how she'd missed the feel of him against her. Even when things were bad between them, she'd loved the slide of his skin on hers. Loved the sensation of stroking her fingers through the mat of dark hair in the middle of his chest. For weeks, she'd thought about nothing else but getting back into Dev's bed.

And now she didn't want to wait another minute.

"Take me now, Dev," she whispered, going up on her toes as he bent his head to taste her breast. "I need you so much...."

He raised his head, looking down at her through blue eyes glazed with a passion she'd spent weeks dreaming of seeing. "This isn't how I planned tonight," he admitted, his voice rough with a tightly controlled need.

"Does it matter?" she asked and lifted one hand to let her fingertips trail from his collarbone down to his flat abdomen.

He shivered, closed his eyes, then opened them again to stare directly into hers. "No. It doesn't."

"I want you," she said softly, watching his eyes, gauging his reaction to her words. "I want you inside me. I want to feel you, hard and deep."

His eyes flashed and Val took a deep breath, luxuriating in the knowledge that her husband, the man she loved, could be so hungry for her. He might not love her yet, but desire was a good place to start. If he felt only half of what she was feeling, then she knew she could win his love. Knew she'd convince him that what had begun as a marriage of convenience on his side could become what all marriages should be. A match of love.

"Hold on," he muttered, then bent, scooped her into his arms and carried her across the wide room, down the short hall and into his bedroom. He paused on the threshold and Valerie turned to see the room as he was seeing it.

She'd prepared for this night in here, too. Dozens of candles flickered around the room, their dancing flames casting shadows of light and movement on the walls. The patio doors were open to the night and the soft song of the cool wind slid into the room, caressing heated skin.

The duvet was turned back, displaying dark red sheets, and the pillows were plumped in invitation.

He turned his gaze down to hers and smiled briefly, one corner of his mouth tipping up. "You've been busy."

"Yes," she said, lifting one hand to trace that slight smile with the tip of her finger. "And I've been waiting for you for hours."

"Waiting's over," he told her. "For both of us."

Then he carried her into the room, eased her down onto the mattress and stood back long enough to strip the rest of his clothes off. Val's breath caught in her chest as she stared up at the man who had claimed so much of her heart and mind for months.

His chest was sculpted and tanned. His legs were powerful, muscular, and his erection was immense. Before, she'd been terrified by the size of him. Now, she took another breath and fought down the first signs of trepidation to rear their ugly heads that night. She remembered the pain of their first joining and couldn't help wincing at the memory. But that was then, she told herself as he leaned over her. This is now. And tonight would be different, because *she* was different.

She wasn't going to lie back and be made love to. She was going to be an active participant.

Dev's gaze was locked on hers and Val saw the hesitation there even before he asked, "Are you sure?"

"Yes," she said, making her voice firm enough to convince not only him, but herself. Nerves were willed into the background and passion was given complete control. This wasn't the time for thinking. Here, in his arms, she wanted only to feel.

"Good," he said and took her mouth with his even as his left hand swept down her body to cup her heat.

Valerie nearly came off the mattress as his fingers and

thumb stroked her inner core, driving her closer and closer to a ragged edge of sanity. Sensation after sensation crowded into her system as she felt herself tightening into a coiled spring that was sure to explode any second.

Magic, she thought again, her mind fogging over as Dev's tongue tangled with hers, his breath sliding into her lungs. Here was what she'd dreamed of.

Her hips arched off the bed as she moved into his hand, again and again, rocking against him, whimpering from the back of her throat as he pushed first one finger, then two, into her depths. It felt so good. So right. So…amazing.

His thumb brushed over the most sensitive spot on her body, sending electrical-like jolts of something incredible spinning off through her system only to slide back and build into another crescendo. He tore his mouth from hers, shifted position slightly and took first one of her nipples and then the other into his mouth.

His lips and tongue and teeth tormented her while his magic fingers continued to push her higher and faster than she'd ever been before. With so many feelings trapped inside, Val could hardly breathe.

She opened her eyes and watched candle-flame shadows dance on the ceiling until Dev raised his head and moved to block her view. Then all she could see were his eyes. The passion. The hunger, staring back down at her. His jaw tight, his breath hissing from his lungs, he was a man so tightly strung she couldn't imagine the control he was wielding.

But she didn't want him controlled. She wanted him as wild as she. Wanted him to feel what she felt. To experience the raging pulse of sensation that he was providing her.

Val tried to tell him that, tried to speak, but words wouldn't come as her body exploded under the frantic ministrations of his hand. Sparks of brilliant color flashed in her mind as her hips rocked and she mindlessly moved into what he offered, seeking more.

She'd had no idea. None. She'd expected that sex could be great, though her experience up until tonight hadn't been fabulous. But this was something else. Something she couldn't have been prepared for. This was *everything*.

"Now," he whispered in her ear as he shifted position, kneeling between her legs, pushing his hard, thick body into hers inch by delectable inch.

She felt the pressure of his gentle invasion and this time instead of fighting it, she welcomed it, spreading her thighs wider, lifting her hips to take him deeper. And when he was settled completely within her, she took one moment to relish the sense of rightness that rushed through her.

This is what she'd been missing. What they'd *both* missed.

Val looked up into his eyes as he rocked his hips against her and she saw his dark blue gaze go even darker as passion claimed him and drew him into the same vortex that held her so tightly in its grasp. They moved together—finally, together—in an ancient dance performed by lovers for centuries.

Here was the magic.

Here was the hunger.

Here was where she belonged.

In his arms.

Val locked her legs around his hips and held him tighter, deeper, as his pulse raced, his breath came short and fast. Amazingly enough, she felt her own body's climb to release again. It started deep within her and mounted every time Dev moved inside her. Stroking, caressing, claiming.

And this time, when her climax slammed into her, Dev was there with her. He called her name out low as he followed her into that mind-numbing world where sensation is king.

Four

Stunned, Dev fought for breath, looked down into Val's eyes and felt himself getting lost in those wild, violet depths. She smiled up at him and ran her fingers down the side of his face, and he could have sworn he felt that gentle touch right down to his bones.

She'd shaken him, loathe as he was to admit it.

To avoid those thoughts, Dev rolled to one side of her and lay staring blankly up at the ceiling. Heart pounding, body still humming, he had to admit that she'd shocked him completely. He couldn't even remember the last time anyone had taken him unawares.

Turning his head, he looked at her and, in the candlelight, her skin looked like gold, her eyes were soft and her mouth—her incredible mouth—was curved into a self-satisfied smile.

Proud of herself, was she?

Well, damn, she had a right to be. Never in his life had he come so close to losing himself so completely in a woman. Always before, there'd been that silent presence in his mind, warning him to maintain control. Tonight, he'd had to *fight* for that control. Tonight, the woman who was his wife had nearly brought him to his knees.

This was *not* the Valerie Shelton Hudson he had married. He'd known something had changed that afternoon, when she'd faced him down in her condo and delivered her list of conditions before agreeing to come home. The woman he'd known before had been shy; timid, really. Never venturing an opinion, never opening herself up to confrontation.

She'd changed in the time they'd been apart. Somehow, she'd come into her own, found a backbone and a sense of self. Or had she always possessed those attributes and had simply been hiding them? But why would she have done that? That didn't make sense.

God, his brain was too fractured to figure any of this out tonight. His body was still reeling from spectacular sex and his lungs were busy trying to draw in enough air to sustain him.

She'd blindsided him.

Seeing her waiting for him—naked—Dev hadn't been able to think beyond his own needs. He doubted he'd be able to get that image of her out of his mind anytime soon, either. But having her match the needs pounding through his body with a desire he'd never experienced from her before had only fed the fires consuming him.

This, Devlin hadn't counted on.

He'd optimistically hoped that he and Val could find a way to live together with some semblance of a decent sex life. He'd thought that he'd spend the next few weeks easing her past her fears and awakening her to her sensuous side.

He'd never considered that what he might find with Val could leave him shaken.

But even as that thought shot through his mind again, Dev dismissed it. He wasn't really shocked. Just surprised, he reassured himself. Happily surprised.

But this tenuous new connection he had with Val was not going to intrude on his life. He'd asked her to marry him for sensible, logical reasons that were still valid. He wouldn't allow his heart to be involved. Better to stay as remote as possible. Yet...

"What are you thinking?"

"What? Oh. Nothing."

Val turned into him, pillowed her head on his chest and wriggled in until she was comfortable. Dragging the tips of her fingers across his chest, she sighed. "That was incredible, Dev. Didn't you feel it?"

God, he thought. Why did women always want to *talk* after sex? What was it that drove them to dissect whatever had happened, talk about their feelings and then ask about *his?*

"Sure," he said in as noncommittal a fashion as he could before tipping his head down to look at her. She was staring at him with stars in her eyes, and Dev could almost feel the ground beneath him lurch and tremble.

Her cheeks were flushed; her deep, violet eyes were shining and her mouth was still puffy from his kisses. She looked absolutely edible. And as he felt his body stir, he knew he hadn't had enough of this surprising woman.

"I had no idea it could be like that," she said, still a little breathless.

"Neither did I." The words were out before he could censor them.

"So you did feel something special—"

Through talking, Dev found a way to distract both of them. He cupped one of her breasts in his palm and lazily stroked the tip of her nipple. She sucked in a gulp of air, closed her eyes and released that breath on a sigh.

"That feels so…"

"Yes, it does," he finished for her. And suddenly, ending a conversation was the last thing on his mind. He wanted to taste her again. To take his time and explore his wife's tempting body. So he stopped any further questions by taking her mouth with his.

Instantly, a rush of heat rose up inside him and staggered Dev with the force of his reaction to her. Only moments ago, he'd been finished, damn near destroyed by the power of their lovemaking—and now he couldn't wait to be inside her again.

Passion roared more ferociously than before and Dev surrendered to it. His tongue parted her lips and as he tasted her warmth, she wrapped her arms around his neck and held his head to her, giving as good as she got. When she sighed, he felt a twinge of something he didn't want to identify. So he ignored it and concentrated on the woman in his arms.

He might be keeping his heart out of this, but that didn't mean he couldn't revel in the pleasure they found together. Dev dragged Val over him until she was sprawled on top of him. Her hair fell on either side of her face like a soft, sweet-smelling brown curtain.

She smiled down at him as he ran his hands up and down her back and Dev felt again that nudge of something inside. But he closed it off, barricaded it behind the wall of control he'd spent years building and instead concentrated solely on the feel of her in his arms. Her eager response was open and trusting and made him even more grateful that she'd somehow found a way to overcome her shyness.

"You amaze me," he said before he could stop himself.

She grinned suddenly and braced herself on his chest, looking down at him as if she'd discovered some glorious secret that she was keeping to herself.

"I'm glad, Dev," she said softly just before she leaned in to brush another kiss against his lips. "I'm so very glad."

Then she went up on her knees and slowly, incredibly slowly, lowered herself onto him. Where the hell was she finding all of this sensual bravado? And why did he care? Devlin grabbed her hips, hissed in a breath and his gaze locked on hers, forgot everything but what she was doing to him.

His shy little wife was gone and in her place was the kind of woman who could haunt a man's dreams.

Nothing mattered more than the next moment, the next slide of her body onto his. She arched her back, moaned his name, and he was caught in the glory of her.

She swayed and the candlelight caressed her skin. The pearls at her throat gleamed with what looked like a soft, inner light. She moved on him, her body taking his deeper, higher, until Dev couldn't form a single thought that wasn't about her.

And as she shuddered over him, riding the crest of her release, he let himself go, the ragged edges of his control nearly sliding from his grasp.

By the next morning, though, his blood had cooled and his brain was back in charge. Now, Dev was ready to consider what might be motivating Val's complete personality turnaround. Who was this new version of his wife? Was this who she really was, or was it all an act designed to snare him into sexual submission?

As that thought shot through his mind, Dev snorted at his own wild imaginings. He was making her sound Machiavellian. She wasn't, he assured himself, though doubts still clanged in his mind like warning bells. If she did have an ulterior motive for this sexy new persona, what could it possibly be?

He glanced at her sleeping in his bed and fought the urge to join her there. He'd never spent a night like the one he'd just lived through and a part of him hadn't wanted it to end.

Valerie had shown him a side of her he hadn't known existed. Now that he knew, now that he'd experienced something he'd never found with anyone else, he wasn't sure what to do about it. Of course, the only real option was to continue on as he'd always been. Cool. In control. There was no reason he couldn't enjoy the nights in his wife's arms and still maintain the distance he required in a relationship.

She sighed in her sleep and rolled over, dragging the red sheet up higher on her shoulder. The contrast of the rich, silky material against her pale, smooth skin jolted something inside him. Something he didn't care to explore.

Frowning, he told himself it was enough that she was back here. Where she belonged. Soon, they'd ease into a routine. A calm, organized marriage of mutual respect and shared pleasures. Just the way it should be.

As long as he remembered who was in control.

"No problem," he whispered. Smiling to himself, and already thinking about the night to come, Dev headed out, quietly closing the bedroom door behind him. He glanced toward the balcony where the remnants of their dinner remained on the table and told himself not to remember how they'd eaten dessert.

If he allowed himself to think about the chocolate raspberry mousse and just how good it had tasted when licked from Val's abdomen, he wouldn't be able to walk. Blowing out a breath, he shook his head and strode to the door.

Rather than taking the private entrance from his suite, he went down the double-wide staircase. He wanted to talk to his father before leaving for work, which meant hunting Markus down at breakfast.

Dev's shoes clicked against the marble floor and echoed weirdly with the fifteen-foot ceilings as he hit the bottom of the stairs and stepped into the foyer.

"Morning, Mr. Hudson." One of the maids was already at work, polishing the hall tables.

"Good morning, Ellen." He kept walking, moving down the long, marble-tiled hallway. Dev barely noticed anymore the hand-painted wallpaper or the antiquities his parents had collected during their travels over the years. The Hudson family home was old, stately and elegant, from the formal dining room to the front salon where guests were lavishly entertained. Not exactly kid-friendly, though he and his brothers and sister had run wild through the place when they were young.

But as refined as the public areas of the house were, the back half of the house was for family.

There was, of course, a private screening room, where the Hudsons could gather to watch films—both the ones made by their company and others, to keep up on the competition. But the family room was filled with bookshelves, a pool table and a bar where they could all relax. The kitchen was huge and airy, with a connected breakfast room, where the family usually tried to have Sunday brunch together. A chance for all of them to catch up on the latest news, which lately, he thought grimly, hadn't been worth talking about.

With the bombshells that had landed in the middle of the Hudson clan in the last couple of months, the family was mostly in defense mode. Circling the wagons. Holding together as a united front.

Which was one of the main reasons Dev had wanted Val to come back to him. Especially with the Academy Awards coming up in just a couple of short weeks. The more the newspapers and tabloids saw that the Hudson family were together in this, the better.

Of course, it was hard to look united, he thought, when his own mother had slipped out of the family mansion to hole up in the penthouse suite at the Chateau Marmont.

He pushed that thought out of his mind because if he started thinking about everything his mother had done to sink this family, he'd need a drink and it was way too early for that.

Dev found Markus Hudson in the family breakfast room, reading the morning paper. A pale wash of early morning sunlight sifted in through the wide windows and lay across the pale oak table.

"Anything interesting, Dad?" he asked and moved to the sideboard where a pot of coffee waited. He poured himself a cup and carried it to the table.

"The usual," Markus said with a smile as he set the paper aside. His dark brown hair was liberally streaked with silver, and his brown eyes were shrewd. As the CEO of Hudson Pictures, Markus had his finger on the pulse of the studio and didn't miss much. "You're up early."

He *was* early. Even for him. But Devlin hadn't wanted to risk having to "talk" to Val before having a chance to do some thinking. But no way was he going to say that to his father. So he shrugged. "A few things I want to check on at the studio."

"Problems?" his father asked, leaning back in his chair, all attention focused on his son.

The last thing he wanted to do was give his father more to worry about. "No, not really, but I wanted to tell you before I handle the situation."

Instantly, Markus went on alert and Dev admired that ability. Most of his life, he'd striven to be as much like his father as he could.

"What's going on?"

Dev smiled, enjoying this quiet time with his father. "The usual. Harrow's gone way over budget on location and I'm going to tell him to pull it back or I'll pull the plug on the film."

Markus laughed, clearly enjoying that image. "That will make you popular."

Wryly, Dev nodded. As the chief money man of Hudson Pictures, he was often the target of bitter directors and furious actors. But what none of them seemed to remember was that making movies was a *business* first. Sure, the art of the thing was important. But if he wasn't controlling the financial aspect of everything, then there wouldn't be any art, would there?

"Do what you have to do, Dev," his father said, reaching for his coffee cup. "I trust you."

"Thanks." That trust was something Dev worked hard to honor. In fact, trust was everything. Without it…well, they already knew what happened when *faith* was broken. Sabrina Hudson had broken faith with everything the Hudson family had stood for. She'd betrayed Markus and just thinking about it made everything inside Dev cold and hard and filled with resentment.

His own mother had cheated on his father. The "perfect" marriage he and his siblings had always held up as the measuring stick of all relationships had been fractured years ago and then covered up in secrecy. It was amazing that the truth hadn't been revealed long ago. But what if it had been, he wondered. Would Markus and Sabrina have divorced? Would Dev and the others have grown up shuttling between parents as so many other children in Hollywood did?

He hated this. Dev looked at his father and realized the man looked older than he had just a month or so ago. Treachery, and grief over Lillian's death wasn't good for the soul, apparently. Plus, Dev's grandmother had died recently and his father was still reeling from it. And another tide of resentment toward his mother washed through Dev. His father hadn't spoken against his wife and Dev hadn't brought the subject up, not wanting to make things even harder on the older man.

But though he was furious with his mother for her betrayal, there was a part of Dev that wanted to go to her. Talk to her. Ask her how in the hell she could have done something so hideous to all of them.

It wasn't just her husband she'd betrayed. She'd lied to *all* of them for years, simply by pretending nothing had happened. That everything was as it should be. And she'd lied about his sister Bella's parentage. Hell, Bella was only just now recovering from the shock of discovering that the man she'd considered her uncle was, in fact, her father.

David Hudson, Markus's brother, had made himself scarce since the scandal had broken, but that was hardly surprising. Any bastard who would sleep with his brother's wife wouldn't be man enough to stick around after he'd caused so much pain.

"Dev," his father said tightly, "you've got to let the anger go."

"What?" He blinked, shook his head and stared at his father.

"I can see by the look on your face what you're thinking about." Markus held his coffee cup and tapped one finger against the porcelain edge.

"I don't know what you're—"

"Save it," Markus said. "You don't have a poker face, Dev. I've always been able to read you like a book."

True. But it had nothing to do with a poker face. The reason Markus could read Dev was because they were so much alike. And maybe that was why his mother's cheating had hit Dev especially hard. He was like his father. So in choosing to step away from her husband, Sabrina had also chosen to step back from her oldest son. And that cut dug deep whether he wanted to admit it or not.

"Sorry," he muttered, taking a sip of the too-hot coffee and burning his tongue for his trouble.

"Don't be." Markus sat forward, leaned his elbows on the glossy, mahogany dining table and looked at his son. "Do you think I don't know you're in pain, too? That all of you haven't been affected by this?"

"It's not about us," Devlin tried to say.

"The hell it's not," Markus countered. "I don't want any of you being angry at your mother over this."

Dev snorted. "A little late for that, Dad."

"Well, get over it."

"I'm sorry?"

"You heard me." Markus set his cup down onto the saucer with a quiet clatter. "Yes, this has upset the whole family and you're all involved...especially Bella." He paused, swallowed hard and shook his head as if to push away disturbing thoughts. "But Sabrina's your mother and you owe her respect."

"Respect."

"That's right." His father's eyebrows lowered over narrowed eyes. "You four are her children. You don't have the right to sit in judgment of her."

Dev snorted.

His father glared at him. "What's between me and my wife, we'll settle ourselves. You don't know everything, Dev. You couldn't. None of you can. Your mother and I have things to resolve and we will. In our own time. Our children don't get a vote in any of it no matter how much we both love you all."

A little stunned, Dev looked at his father. He hadn't expected Markus to defend Sabrina, though he should have. His whole life his parents had been, seemingly, happy. Sure, his father had been devoted to his work, as Dev was, but a child can tell when his parents love each other. That had never been in doubt. Which was why all of this had been such a blow to the family. "You've spoken to Mom?"

Markus sighed. "Of course I've spoken to her, and that's my point, Dev. Whatever happens between your mother and me is between your mother and me."

He understood that. On a purely rational, logical level. But the truth was, what he was feeling had nothing to do with logic or rationality.

This was about lies.

Lies she'd told.

Lies she'd lived.

And the pain of realizing his mother was not the woman he'd always thought her to be was something Dev was having a hard time accepting. But he wasn't going to cause his father even more grief by arguing with the man.

"You're right, Dad," he said, draining what was left of his cooling coffee.

"Glad that's settled. Now, was there anything else you needed to talk to me about?"

Dev thought about it for a moment, then decided there was no point in keeping Val's return a secret. "Yeah, there is. Not work-related, though. Val's back in the mansion."

"Really?" Markus smiled, reached out and slapped his oldest son on the shoulder. "That's wonderful news. I'm glad you two worked things out. Your mother will be…"

His voice trailed off, and Devlin scowled. Everything came back to Sabrina and the rift her actions had caused in the family. By rights his mother should be here. At the house. Instead, she was staying in a hotel, leaving her husband here alone.

God, how had this happened to them?

The Hudsons had always been the anti-Hollywood family. Strong. United. Untouched by the scandals and the troubles that seemed to fester in this city. He'd always thought they'd been blessed, somehow. Apparently though, the warranty on "blessed" had run out.

Dropping all mention of his mother, Dev said, "Look, I've got to get hold of Harrow and stop him before he spends another week on the location shoot. He should be able to do interiors at the studio and he can CG whatever else he needs in postproduction."

"Harrow won't like that," Markus warned with a knowing smile. "He's an 'artist.' Just ask him, he'll tell you."

Glad to be back on safer ground, Dev smiled at his father. "He may be an artist, but I'm the man with his hands on the money. So Harrow will listen. He won't like it but he'll listen."

Standing up, he buttoned his suit jacket and headed for the door. His personal life might be filled with questions at the moment, Dev told himself, but at least he could still lose himself in work.

Five

Valerie woke up alone. Somehow, after the night before, she'd expected to be awakened by a husband who wanted to rekindle the fires they'd discovered. A tiny twist of worry settled in her stomach as she wondered if Dev had already dismissed her from his mind. But she quickly resolved that if he *had* put last night behind him already, she would soon remind him of everything.

She wasn't going to be ignored this time around.

And in that spirit, she spent the morning figuring out how she could change things up in their wing of the mansion. If she wasn't going to get a home of her own just yet, then she was going to make sure Dev realized that he was now *sharing* this apartment.

There wasn't much she could do about the big stuff

until she'd had time to see a decorator and go shopping. But she wanted to get a jump on as much as she could. Really all she was trying to do at the moment was make a statement. Something subtle, to let Dev know that this was a brand-new day. That she was his wife and she was a part of his life, not just an incidental appendage.

Then naturally, her mind drifted to the night before. She slid her gaze to the balcony beyond the open French doors. The housekeeping staff had already been through, clearing away the remnants of their late-night dinner. But the memories were with Val for life. Just thinking about the cold chill of chocolate raspberry mousse hitting her heated skin made her shiver all over again. Her husband could be very…inventive. She smiled to herself, delighted so far with her second chance at marriage.

"But sex is just the beginning," she whispered, reassuring herself that she would have more than a mattress as the basis of her life. "All I have to do is show him how much he needs me. And he *does* need me. He's too alone. Too shut off." She frowned a little, then added, "But not for long."

Now if only she had a touch more muscle.

The chairs in the main room were heavier than they looked and thumped heavily against the floor when she shoved at them. Well, moving them an inch at a time was going to take a year at least.

Out of breath and getting seriously irritated, she was grateful when a knock sounded on the door outside Dev's room. She whipped her hair back out of her eyes, glared at the ugly brown chair that was fighting to hold its ground and then yanked open the door.

"Val! You *are* back! This is great! Dad told me you were, but I just had to see it for myself. And I'm so glad!" Bella Hudson sailed into the apartment, her expensive perfume trailing in her wake. Her auburn hair hung in thick, lush waves around her shoulders and her blue eyes were sparkling with humor. She wore a dark green silk shirt, skintight blue jeans and a pair of gold sandals.

To complete the package, tucked into the curve of her arm was Bella's favorite accessory, her dog, Muffin. With tangled, wiry hair, a pushed-in face and crooked teeth, the fifteen-pound dog was friendly, but possibly the ugliest canine in the known universe. Today, Muffin was wearing a T-shirt the very same color as Bella's blouse.

Val hid a smile and closed the door behind Dev's sister. "It's so good to see you."

Over the last couple of months, her sister-in-law had been through some pretty ugly times. Every paper in the country had been blaring the long-kept secret that Bella Hudson was not Markus's daughter after all, but the result of an affair between her mother and Markus's brother, David. And though Val's heart had hurt for Bella, she hadn't been able to talk to her, offer support.

Mainly because the moment the story broke, Bella had run to France, trying to distance herself from nosy reporters and photographers. No doubt she'd also been trying to come to grips with the news herself.

It didn't help the situation any that Val had left Dev just after Bella's world dissolved. Now they were both back at Hudson Manor and both trying to rebuild their lives. Of course, Bella was ahead of Val on that score.

She was madly in love with her fiancé, Sam Garrison, and lucky for her, Sam felt the same way.

Briefly, Val sighed inwardly, hoping that one day, she'd know how it felt to love and be loved in return.

Then Bella wrapped Val in a tight, one-armed hug, stepped back and gave her a good looking over. "You look different." She tipped her head to one side. "What is it?"

Did good sex actually show on your face? Val wondered, just a little embarrassed to think that might be true. It was one thing to discover your sexy side and quite another to have the whole world clued in.

So she shrugged and said, as casually as she could, "Nothing different, you're just looking through happy eyes."

"So true. I *really* am." Bella set Muffin down onto the hardwood floor so the dog could wander around and sniff everything in reach. Standing up again, Bella did a quick spin in place. "It's amazing, Val, but a couple of months ago, I was sure my life was over, and now…"

"Better?" Val asked.

"Oh you wouldn't even *believe* how much better."

"How is Sam?" Sam Garrison had clearly made a wonderful difference in the woman's life. She was practically glowing.

"Fabulous." Bella grinned, both eyebrows rising into high arches as she teased, "Been reading the papers, have you?"

"Yes." Valerie dragged her friend over to the closest sofa and once they were seated, she said, "How else could I keep up with my friends?"

Instantly, Bella's smile faded and a guilty expression

flashed across her face. "Oh, honey, I so should have called you, but everything's been so nuts and—"

"No," Val brushed away her friend's concern. She more than anyone else could understand how things could pile up around you until you felt as though you couldn't see straight anymore. "Don't worry about it. I know just what you mean, anyway. I wanted to call you after—"

Bella frowned and chewed at her bottom lip, clearly remembering how crazy things had been when the scandal concerning her parentage broke. "It's probably better that you didn't. I wasn't really good company."

"I know. But you're here now, at the house, so you've made up with—"

Bella shook her head. "I came to see my *father.*" She emphasized the word as if making sure Val knew that she still considered Markus her real father.

And who could blame her? Markus was the one who'd loved her, raised her, worried over her. If that wasn't a father, what was? David Hudson might have contributed the DNA to Bella's makeup, but Markus would always be her father.

"And your mom?" Val leaned forward, laid her hand over Bella's and squeezed.

"We haven't talked yet, but we will soon. We have to. It's just that I don't even know what to feel, you know? I mean, I love Mom, that doesn't change. But how could she have kept this a secret from me? I know I have to talk to her, hear her side of this," she admitted. "I'm still so confused over all of it and I'm not sure if talking to Mom is the best thing to do right now, so…" She glanced around to check on her dog. "Baby, don't chew Uncle Dev's shoe."

Valerie glanced over the back of the sofa and winced. Too late. The Ferragamo loafer was already toast. Shrugging, she thought it served Dev right for leaving them out.

"You know," Bella said brightly, obviously ready for a change in subject, "I'm so tired of talking and thinking about my own weird problems. Tell me about you instead. What brought you back to the Fortress of Solitude?"

Good description of Dev's suite, Val thought, and only a sister would have nailed it so completely. "Your brother."

Bella blinked. "Seriously? He came and got you?"

"Is that so surprising?"

"Are you kidding?" Bella curled her legs up under her, laughed and called out, "Muffin, baby, Uncle Dev won't like it if you tear that book." Then she turned back to Val, still laughing. "The great Devlin Hudson went out of his way to chase down the wife who walked out on him?"

Valerie cringed a little. "Isn't there a nicer way to put that?"

"Nope and don't you dare try," Bella told her with a grin. "It's just what Dev needed. A good solid kick in the pants. And clearly it worked! He went after you! It's historic, that's what it is."

"Bella…" Val couldn't help smiling.

"I mean it! Dev has *never* gone after *any* woman." She shook her head and sounded disgusted with her entire gender as she added, "Women have been throwing themselves at Dev since he was a kid. So the fact that he went after you—why, it's amazing, really."

Thinking about the legions of women who would gladly change places with her didn't fill Val's heart with glee, but at the same time, maybe Bella had a point. He *had* come to her. He *had* been the one to suggest giving their marriage another chance. Maybe she had a better shot at winning her husband's love than she'd thought.

"And thank heaven you agreed to come back to him," Bella said. "He's been the most awful bear of a person to be around since you left."

"Really?" Oh, that made her feel better. She'd hate to think she had been the only one miserable when they were apart.

"Oh, totally. He was so mad when you left, nobody wanted to talk to him. Even his assistant walked a wide berth around him and Megan Carey's not afraid of anybody."

That small spark of pleasure inside her quickly sputtered out of existence. She'd been hoping to hear that Dev had been lonely, missing her, even maybe heartbroken. Instead, he'd simply been angry. "So he wasn't miserable; he was pissed."

"He was both, trust me. Dev's not used to losing. At anything. When you left, he was so stunned, all he could handle was anger for a few weeks. Then the misery kicked in." Bella gloated for a second, then frowned, clucked her tongue and said, "Muffin, sweetie pie, you shouldn't sleep on that pillow, I think it's silk."

Valerie glanced over her shoulder and almost applauded as Muffin settled in on one of Dev's hideous brown pillows. When the ugly little dog started nibbling at the corner of the pillow, Valerie could have hugged her.

"Anyway," Bella was saying, "Honestly, Val, I've never seen my brother so…down. I mean he's never been Mr. Sunshine, God knows, but this was a new level of low. You know Dev, always on the even keel. Nothing gets to him. Nothing pushes him over that icy edge of control. Well, until *you*. I think you really shocked the hell out of him when you walked out."

"That's not why I left." Though it was a small comfort to know that she'd finally reached him. Yet how ironic was it that being *with* Dev hadn't melted his reserve—only leaving him had done the trick?

"Honey, I know that." Bella gave her an understanding smile. "Remember, I grew up with the Hudsons. And as much as I love them, that doesn't mean I don't see their faults. And Dev's got more than his share."

Funny, but Valerie felt like defending her husband. Which was just silly, since she basically agreed with his sister's opinion. But even with those faults, Devlin was more of a man than any other Val had ever known. And the only man she'd ever loved.

Which told her he was worth fighting for.

"Oh, I know he's stubborn and arrogant and too closed off," Val said. "But underneath all that, I think he's an amazing man. I really do. All I have to do is convince him how much he needs me."

"You're right, you know," Bella said, smiling, "he *does* need you. Desperately. But just like every other man in the world, he can't see what's right in front of his face. I have faith in you, though. If anyone can get to my stubborn brother, it's you. I think you're perfect for him. Especially now," she added, tilting her head and studying Val carefully. "You seem more…sure of yourself than you were before. Sort of more self-confident."

"Good, I'm glad it shows." Val leaned back into the

sofa. "Before, I was so in love with Dev, I just wanted everything to be perfect, you know?"

"Oh yeah."

"I didn't argue with him, didn't venture an opinion, didn't even stand my ground when he tried to roll right over me."

"He does do that," Bella said with an understanding nod.

"Exactly," Val said and looked around the clearly masculine room, pausing to admire the crystal vase full of the sterling roses Dev had brought her the night before. Then she shifted her gaze back to Bella. "The first time I moved in here, I was so busy trying to be Dev's *wife,* I forgot to be *Val.* But that's not going to happen again."

"Yay, you!"

Valerie grinned and enjoyed the feeling of solidarity with Bella. It was good to have a friend who understood what you were talking about. Who was on your side.

"You know, when we got married, I'm not even sure I knew what I wanted, besides Dev, of course. But now…" She shifted her gaze back to her friend and her husband's sister, "Now I want it all."

"No point in going for half," Bella agreed. "God knows I wouldn't settle for less than all of Sam, so you've got my vote."

"Thanks. I appreciate that."

Bella smiled. "So, what were you up to in here when I showed up?"

"Well, I *was* trying to move this furniture around. You know, just shake things up a little. But it's so darn heavy, I can't really budge it."

"Wondered what that thumping I heard was about," Bella mused, glancing around the big room with the sunlight spilling through the French doors. "Hmm. You're right. This room *is* frozen in time. Dev probably hasn't moved a thing since he moved into this wing years ago."

Just what Val had suspected. Well then, it was way past time for a change, wasn't it? "You know, if I had a little help, I could probably move this furniture. So, do you have some time? Can you help me shift things around?"

Bella laughed. "You *do* know we could call downstairs and get plenty of help in an instant."

"Yeah..." Val said, not wanting to do that. If she was going to show Dev that she was a brand-new woman, then she was going to do this by herself. Well, with Bella, if she'd help.

"You want to do it," the other woman said softly.

"Yes, I do."

"Then we'd better get started," Bella told her, pushing up from the sofa. "Oh, Muffin, honey, do you have to go potty?" Then a moment later, she glanced at Val with an apologetic shrug. "You were going to get rid of that ugly pillow anyway, right?"

"Definitely," Val told her, looking at the spot where Muffin had apparently lost the fight to control her bladder.

"Okay, then, no loss." Bella grinned. "Where do we start?"

Val stood up, looked around and sighed. "For right now, let's just shake up the furniture arrangement. These deliberate little conversation areas give me chills."

Bella laughed. "Really. If you have to *tell* people to have conversations, what's the point?"

"This is gonna be fun," Val said. "Let's start by sliding this sofa over there by the fireplace."

"Excellent." Bella positioned herself at one end of the big couch. "Good thing there are hardwood floors. We can slide these monsters around."

Val thought briefly about the condition of the gleaming floors, then dismissed the notion of scrapes and scratches. She'd just have them redone. Or buy colorful rugs. Or maybe carpet…God, the possibilities were endless.

"I can see you imagining all sorts of different things," Bella mused.

"Am I that obvious?"

"Only to me and that's only because I care about you. And Dev. So my fingers are crossed for you." Bella smiled at her and Val felt a rush of warmth for the sister-in-law who had become a friend.

With support like this, Val thought her chances of winning Dev over were much improved. She knew how close the Hudson siblings were. When the scandal about Bella's birth had been leaked to the press, the woman's brothers had figuratively circled the wagons to protect her from as much hurt as they could.

"Thanks, Bella. I appreciate it. Because frankly, I think I'm going to need all the help I can get."

"Oh, I don't know." Bella straightened up, gave a knowing look to the roses and smiled. "Seems to me you've got his attention already."

"True. It's *keeping* it that's got me worried."

"Not going to be a problem. I think you're perfect for Dev. Just don't give up on him. He's going to be a lot of work, but he's so worth it. He's a good man, Val. Keep reminding yourself of that," Bella said.

"Don't worry," Val told her and bent over to get a good grip on her end of the sofa. "I'm not leaving again. This time, I'm staying."

"Atta girl." Bella blew out a breath. "So, you ready to push this monstrosity into position?"

"More than ready," Val said, knowing she was talking about much more than rearranging furniture. She was up to the challenge of rebuilding her life and dragging Dev right along with her.

"You can't do this to me," Dave Harrow shouted and tore at his already sparse gray hair. "I need another three days, at least, on location. I can't be expected to shoot this movie completely in studio."

Dev wasn't moved by the histrionics. If there was one thing Hollywood directors were good at, it was drama. Hell, there should be an Academy Award category for drama-queen directors who had more of a lock on acting than the young actors who caused so many young women to dream happy dreams.

"Look, Harrow," Dev told him, drawing the man away from the crowd so clearly interested in their conversation. "You're already over budget and you know it. I've bent the rules as far as they're gonna go. So dial it back or see the film shelved."

Harrow's frantic brown eyes slid from side to side, as if looking for someone to come to his rescue. But there was no one. The older man had been doing this long enough to know that Devlin Hudson didn't bluff.

"Fine," he finally grumbled. "We'll wrap the shoot tomorrow and do the rest in studio."

"Today."

Harrow's features flushed a brilliant red and he kicked at the dirt at his feet. "Tomorrow and that's my last offer."

Dev thought about it, hid a smile and let the director think he was winning this round. When the truth was, Dev had already decided on the drive to the location to give the man one more day to wrap things up.

"Fine," he finally said, as if he'd been considering options. "Tomorrow. Then you're done."

"Agreed, you tightfisted, penny-counting bastard."

At that, Dev actually grinned. "Coming from an arrogant, egotistic spendthrift, I take that as a compliment."

"As you should," Harrow grudgingly admitted. "You're a hard man to deal with, but you don't stick your nose in too much, I suppose."

"Harrow," Dev asked with a smile, "does this mean you really, really like me?"

The older man snorted derisively. "That joke's almost as old as you are. Besides, I don't like anybody and you damn well know it." He nodded at the craft services table. "Feel like a cup of coffee before you get the hell out of my hair?"

"You keep yanking at that wild mane and you won't have any left." Dev checked the gold Rolex on his wrist. "Why not? You can complain some more."

Harrow led the way to the catering trucks, set up under a bank of trees near the cliff's edge overlooking Laguna Beach.

A pretty city in Orange County about forty miles outside L.A., it was the perfect location for the outdoor shoot, but that didn't mean that Dev was going to keep authorizing money spent on dragging actors, sets, lights and catering trucks all the way out here.

"You guys in the office don't understand what we have to put up with," Harrow was saying as he stalked toward the promised coffee.

"And you guys behind the cameras always say that," Dev shot back, enjoying himself now. Truth was, Harrow was a damn good director and this movie was sure to be a hit for Hudson Pictures. With its bright young stars, beach location and the best writer in Hollywood, Dev was already calculating a runaway blockbuster.

They'd almost reached the catering trucks when Harrow was sidetracked by an assistant director, so Dev wandered a bit. The sea wind pushed at him as he strolled to the edge of the cliff and looked down on the waves crashing against jagged rocks. It was February, but that didn't stop dozens of surfers from sitting on their boards in the cold, gray Pacific.

There were only a few people strolling the sand and one golden retriever splashed into the water chasing a bright red ball. When his cell phone rang, Dev grumbled. "Take a damn second to relax and see how long it lasts."

He glanced at the screen and everything in him fisted as he recognized a number he hadn't seen on his phone in more than two months. Flipping it open, he said, "Valerie?"

"Hi, Dev, yes, it's me. I wanted to know if you were going to be here for dinner."

The question took him completely by surprise. She'd never before called to ask when he'd be home. Or even *if* he'd be home. She'd actually pretty much tiptoed around him, as if afraid to open her mouth.

Those days, apparently, were gone.

"What?" He shook his head and stared unseeing out at the choppy waves pummeling the beach.

Silence for a moment, then she said, "You know. *Dinner?* The last meal of the day?"

He scowled a bit and absently watched a surfer ride his chosen wave into shore where it dissolved into foam. "I know what it is, I'm just not sure why you—"

"I picked up some amazing scallops at the Farmers Market earlier and I thought I'd make dinner but I wanted to make sure you'd be here on time, otherwise—"

"You're *making* dinner?" he interrupted her and pulled the phone away from his ear briefly to check again on just who was calling him. But it was Valerie. No mistake.

Still, this was a different Val than he remembered. She hadn't once cooked for him since they'd been married. Most often, they'd had meals with the family in the first-floor dining room. Easier all around and frankly, he hadn't been looking for alone time with his too shy and quiet wife.

What in the hell would they have talked about?

Clearly though, those days were long gone. Then memories of the night before swam in his brain and he reminded himself that she was different in a *lot* of areas.

"Yes, I'm cooking. I'm pretty good, too," she argued hotly.

"I didn't say you weren't."

"You were thinking it."

"You read minds now, too?"

"It wasn't hard," she said softly.

Did she sound disappointed, or was that just his imagination?

"So will you be home or not?"

Now she sounded exasperated, and that he was sure he wasn't imagining.

"Yes." He checked his watch, glanced over his shoulder to see the director waiting for him and said, "I'll be there. Should be home by six."

"Excellent."

He could almost *hear* the smile in her voice and he caught himself smiling in response. Then he frowned to himself and wondered why the hell it pleased him to make her happy all of a sudden. But the answer to that question wasn't something he wanted to consider.

"Okay then," Val said, her voice a lot chirpier now, "I'll see you later. Have a good day, Dev."

Then she was gone and he was standing in the windswept sunshine, staring down at his phone as if he'd just lost a connection to Mars.

What in the hell was going on with his wife?

That question stayed buried in the back of his mind even as he walked to meet Harrow and talk movies.

Six

Valerie was lighting pale pink taper candles when she heard Dev's key in the lock. Her breath caught in her chest and instantly, a swarm of bumblebees started doing doughnuts in the pit of her stomach. Stupid, really, to be nervous. But she couldn't help it. She was so determined to win her husband's love that every move she made, she worried if it was the right one.

But she'd already decided on this course, and heaven knew she was prepared for it, so she might as well enjoy the scene she'd set. The candles were flickering lazily in the soft wind dancing across the balcony. Cool jazz was drifting from the stereo. Appetizers were arrayed on the table for two and she was wearing the dress Bella had talked her into buying.

She was as ready as she was going to be.

As the door opened, she hurried into the room to meet him, but before she could call out a greeting, Val heard a sharp thud followed by Dev's yelp.

"Dev?" Hurrying across the shadow-filled room, her high heels sounded out at a fast clip on the hardwood floor. "Are you okay?"

He dropped his keys on the table she'd moved into position that morning then limped toward her. "Once the throbbing stops I'll be fine."

"What did you do?" she asked.

"I nearly killed myself on the damn table that wasn't there when I left for work," he told her, then stopped dead and looked around the room. Dozens of candles threw soft light into a shadowy cavern of a room, but provided just enough illumination for him to see the changes she'd made. "What happened in here? Who moved the furniture?"

"I did."

His gaze slid to hers. *"Why?"*

His blue eyes were narrowed in suspicion and his dark hair was rumpled, as if he'd been dragging his hands through it. His tie was loose at his neck and the collar button of his shirt undone. He looked absolutely incredible. Val's body seemed to light up like a Christmas tree, but she fought the delicious sensations into submission. There'd be time enough later for everything she wanted to do with him.

Right now, he was still waiting for an answer to his question. Valerie gave him a nonchalant shrug, defying the still-swarming bumblebees in her stomach. She'd wanted everything to be perfect when he got home, which just sounded so 1950s TV wifish. Of course, she hadn't considered that Dev would stroll into what he thought was a familiar room and break a leg. Well, she had wondered what his reaction to all her changes might be.

Now she knew. Apparently Dev didn't do well with change. He'd get used to it, she told herself.

"Because we *both* live here now, Dev. And I wanted to shake things up a little."

"A little?" he echoed, then half bent to rub his shin. "I almost killed myself on the table you left by the door."

"Gee," she said with a smile, "you look healthy enough to me."

He shook his head, glancing around the room again, and Valerie followed that movement with her own gaze, loving the layout of the living room now. She'd like it even more once she replaced this ugly brown man-furniture with some nice, overstuffed cozy pieces.

"Looks good, doesn't it?" She pointed. "See, I moved that sofa to face the big-screen TV, but I wanted the other one facing the fireplace. Good for snuggling."

He looked at her. *"Snuggling?"*

She smiled. "And I raided your mom's garden for some fresh flowers. I hope she won't mind...."

"Mom's not here."

"I know, but she'll be back."

He sighed. "Valerie..."

Fine, clearly he didn't want to talk about his mother. She didn't, either. Not at the moment, anyway. "I think you'll like this a lot once you get used to it."

"If the room doesn't kill me first," he muttered. "How did you do all this in one day?"

"Bella helped me."

"Bella was here?"

"This morning," Val said, enjoying the fact that she could surprise him so easily. Tucking her arm through his, she led him farther into the room. "We had a great time."

"I can see that," he muttered, and Valerie's heart sank a little. Was he going to fight her on everything? Was he going to keep making this harder?

Even if he did, she told herself, she wasn't going to stop. She had known going in that this wouldn't be easy. But she was a determined woman. She wanted her husband and she was willing to fight for him—even if that meant making him miserable in the short term.

"So how much do you hate it?" she asked, stopping beside the small, elegantly set table on the balcony. She was becoming very fond of this oh-so-private little patio area. After what she'd experienced there the night before, she'd almost like to see the table bronzed. Heat washed through her at the memories flooding her mind, so to distract herself, she picked up the bottle of cold Chardonnay, poured each of them a glass and handed one to Dev.

In the moonlight, his eyes were shadowed and the emotions she might have seen there were much harder to read.

He took a sip of the wine, blew out a breath and looked at her. "I don't *hate* it. I was just…surprised."

He sort of grimaced on that last word and Val had to wonder why. But then she let that thought go as she noticed his gaze fixed on her. Straightening slightly, Val raised her chin and looked into his eyes. Her skin sizzled with heat as he looked her up and down with a quick, hungry stare. Heartbeat thudding in her chest, she was suddenly very glad she'd gone shopping with Bella that afternoon.

The black dress she wore had a neckline so low, it stopped just short of exposing her nipples. The hem ended right beneath her behind and the narrow shoulder straps were merely a suggestion of black silk. The dress clung to her body like a second skin, so tight in fact, she hadn't been able to wear even a thong because the lines would have shown through. Bella had talked her into buying the dress and Val had been damn near embarrassed just putting it on this afternoon.

But now…with Dev's gaze fixed on her as if he were a starving man and she was the last steak in the world, she felt…powerful.

He took another long sip of wine. "You look—that dress is—"

"You like it?" she asked, doing a slow turn for his benefit. She heard his quick intake of breath as he admired the plunging back and tiny skirt.

"Yeah," he said tightly. "You could say I like it."

"I'm glad."

Her smile was brilliant and Dev felt something inside him lurch, hard and painfully. What the hell was she up to? Was she trying to make him insane? Because if that was the plan, she was doing fine.

Rearranging the furniture, cooking dinner, wearing a dress that made a man want to tear it from her body with his teeth. Lust roared through his system like an out-of-control freight train. He'd done nothing but think about her all day and now there she stood, and he was praying she'd take a breath deep enough to have her breasts pop free of that dress.

God. She'd been home less than forty-eight hours and already she'd tossed his world into complete disorder.

This had *not* been his plan when he'd gone to her condo to bring her home. He was supposed to be the one setting the rules. He was supposed to be the one surprising *her*. Instead, he had the weird sensation of having walked onto a movie set halfway through filming. He didn't know his lines, the plot or any of the twists that Val kept throwing at him.

"Why don't we sit and talk for a while before dinner?" she asked. "When we're ready it'll only take ten minutes for me to cook up the scallops."

Oh, he was ready to eat all right, but dinner was the last thing on his mind. Damn, he was sinking fast here.

"Yeah. That's a good idea." Maybe if he got her talking, he'd be able to figure out just what in the hell she was up to.

"Let's sit on the snuggle sofa, why don't we? Would you mind carrying the wine over while I get these snacks?"

The *snuggle* sofa, for God's sake.

She picked up a silver tray dotted with what looked like delicious appetizers and headed for the couch she'd planted in front of the fireplace that now held only six or seven flickering candles. If he didn't know better, Dev would swear she was deliberately trying to seduce him.

What was she up to?

Devlin's gaze dropped to her behind as she walked away from him and he had to admire the curve of her body caressed in that tight, black material. Then he shook his head to wake himself up and grabbed the bottle of wine. Before he followed her, Devlin glanced at the scene she'd set on the very balcony where they'd made love so frantically the night before.

Candles, fine china, silver ice bucket holding the chilled bottle of wine. The late afternoon breeze was soft and the first stars were just beginning to shine in the dark violet sky.

Funny, but he'd never noticed that the evening sky was the exact color of her eyes.

The minute that thought presented itself, Dev groaned inwardly. Not a good sign, he told himself. Waxing poetic about his wife's eyes, even silently, was a danger sign.

Grumbling to himself, he wondered if she was trying to keep him in such a sexually charged mood that he wouldn't have time to think.

If that was her plan, it was working. Damn it.

His body was tight and hard and uncomfortable and he had the distinct feeling that he'd better get used to it. He carried the wine to the sofa, where she sat waiting for him, legs crossed, eyes shining, welcoming smile on her face.

"Isn't this nicer?" She asked as he sat down beside her. "I love being able to stare into a fire."

"Uh-huh." He slid a glance at her, his gaze dropping to the swell of her breasts, and took an immediate drink of the icy wine, hoping it would help. It didn't.

"Of course, it's too warm tonight for an actual fire, but the candles are good."

"Very nice," he said and heard the tightness in his own voice.

"I think you'll like the furniture arrangement once you get used to it."

"I suppose." He leaned back into the couch, stretched his legs out in front of him and crossed them at the ankle. The scent of her perfume drifted toward him and he instinctively dragged it deep into his lungs.

She was making him crazy.

"Of course, there are a few things I'd like to replace."

"Sure." He paused, thought about it and turned his head to look at her. "What?"

"Well, leather couches aren't really all that comfortable, are they?" She leaned back into the sofa and rested her head on his shoulder.

Her hair was soft and felt cool against his jaw and smelled of flowers and sunshine. Dev took another sip of wine.

"Just don't buy pink, whatever you do," he said. "Bella redid the guest cottage once and there was so much pink it felt like you were walking into cotton candy."

She laughed and he liked the sound of it.

"No pink, I swear."

He smiled, too. It felt…good, sitting here like this, with her, in the shadows, with only the dancing candle flames for light, with the slow slide of jazz whispering into the air. Devlin took another sip of his wine and felt the ragged edges of his hurried day sort of untangle and relax.

Of course, other parts of his body were so far from relaxed he couldn't get comfortable.

"It's a nice night."

"Yeah," he said brusquely. "It is."

She sighed and rubbed her head against his shoulder. "I thought it would be nice to have dinner out on the balcony again. Hope you don't mind…."

"No," he said, quickly shutting down the mental images of their "meal" the night before. "Why would I mind?"

"Good. That's good." He felt her smiling against him. "How was work?"

"How was *work?*"

"Yes," she said and slid her crossed legs against each other in a slow, fluid motion that tore at the edges of Dev's control.

"What are you doing, Val?" He took a big gulp of wine and hardly tasted it as the dry wine slid down his throat.

She sat up straight, raising her head to look directly at him. "What do you mean?"

He waved one arm, encompassing everything she'd done in preparation for his return home. "The wine, the intimate dinner, the questions about my work…what's going on?"

She blinked up at him in wide-eyed innocence. "I don't know what you mean."

Oh, she was good. Much better than he'd given her credit for. They both knew she was playing at something here—and that it was working. So what was the point of denying it? "Yeah, you do."

She sighed, reached down for the bottle of wine and topped off both their glasses. "Dev, I went shopping and wanted to make dinner for you. I bought a new dress I thought you'd like, so I wore it. The weather's gorgeous, so I set the table on the balcony—which you did last night—"

Yes, he thought, but he'd had an ulterior motive for that little dinner.

"And you're my husband," she continued, "so I asked how your day went. If you don't want to talk about it, that's fine, but don't pretend that this is some sort of conspiracy designed to entrap you in some evil plot."

"I didn't mean that," he hedged, knowing he'd meant exactly that.

"Good." She smiled again and used the toe of her high-heeled pump to nudge his left calf. "So why don't you tell me about today."

Oddly defensive now, Dev grabbed at his loosened tie, tore it free and tossed it onto the arm of the sofa. He sat up, handed her his glass and then shrugged out of his suit jacket. Tossing it aside, too, he took his wine from her, had another sip and tried not to notice that in candlelight, her eyes looked like purple velvet. Soft, inviting.

"What do you want to know?"

"Everything," she said, reaching out to lay one hand over his. "What'd you do today?"

Sullenly, he surrendered to the inevitable. Dragging his gaze away from his wife, he leaned back, stared at the candle flames in the hearth and started talking. "I had to go to a location shoot to have a confrontation with a director."

"Mmm. Harrow?"

He shot her a look. "How'd you know that?"

She laughed. "I'm not an idiot, Dev. When we were apart, I didn't stop keeping up with the news. I know Harrow's working on *The Christmas Wish*. I also know that he's legendary for going over budget. It only makes sense that you'd have to go and rein him in."

"Oh." Frowning, he took another sip of wine and felt the cold slide through his system.

"So how did it go?"

Before he knew it, Dev was telling her all about his meeting with the Oscar-winning director. She laughed at his description of the man's temper and then grinned at how easily Dev had defanged the other man.

Encouraged by her interest, he kept talking, telling

her about the rest of his day. She asked intelligent questions, made suggestions for solving problems in ways he wouldn't have considered, and Dev found himself actually relaxing.

He was enjoying this, he realized. He'd never really had anyone but his father or his brothers to bounce ideas off. Bella was too much an artist to want to talk about the nuts and bolts of picture making. And the women he'd dated in the past had been more interested in the glamour of the movie industry than the business of making it run.

But Val, he discovered, had an objective point of view he found refreshing. Something else he'd never expected. She was continuing to surprise him.

But even as he felt himself warming up to her, relaxing in her presence, Devlin heard a warning bell ring in his mind. He couldn't allow himself to be drawn too tightly into her web. He wasn't going to fall in love. Wouldn't make the same mistake his father had.

Look what love had done to *him*. Women couldn't be trusted, he reminded himself. Markus was miserable without Sabrina, despite how he'd defended his wife only that morning—Dev could see that clearly. But how was he supposed to forgive betrayal?

No, Dev would be smarter than his father had been. He'd protect his heart. Keep it safely behind the defensive walls he'd built so well.

"Daddy says you've got a series of ads planned to celebrate *Honor*'s Oscar nominations."

"Yeah," he said tightly, his newly reaffirmed vow fresh in his mind.

"I've been thinking about it and have an idea you might not have considered."

Warily, he asked, "What?"

She smiled and leaned toward him. Dev half expected her breasts to spill out of that dress and couldn't help the pang of disappointment when they didn't.

"I was thinking, every studio in town is running ads touting their movies, but *Honor* is different," she said thoughtfully. "It's a true story."

"Yes, and everyone knows that...."

"Of course people know the basics, but why not remind everyone that this movie is about your family?"

Intrigued, Dev asked, "What did you have in mind?"

She set her glass of wine on the low table in front of them and looked into his eyes. "When you do the ads, promote the reason behind the movie. Remind people— and the Academy voters—that this story is about the Hudsons. Showcase the real story about your grandparents in the ad. Use their photos alongside shots from the movie. Something about the WWII soldier falling in love with the lovely French woman."

While she talked, Dev's mind was racing, seeing possibilities.

"The romance of the story is powerful," Val said, her voice a whisper coated with romance. "Charles and Lillian working together in Nazi-occupied France. His getting wounded, her nursing him back to health. Show their painful separation when he was forced to leave her and their joy when he returned at the war's end."

Dev watched her eyes shine as she spoke and suddenly understood how his grandfather could have been so captivated by a woman that he'd risked everything for her. Valerie was so much more than he'd known. So much more than he'd expected. Her voice, her smile, her scent; she was an assault on the senses from which he might not recover. She made him want. Made him hunger for the touch of her.

"The romance of this story is immense, Dev," she was saying. "It's not just make-believe. It's real. It's the triumph of love during a time of war. It's the real happily ever after that people long for. Remind everyone of just how special their story was."

When she stopped speaking, Dev was still caught in the spell she'd woven and despite the warning bells in his mind, he felt himself falling. There was a breathless silence as she waited for a response from him.

He waited to get a grip on the rushing feelings pouring through him. Finally, hand tight about the stem of the wineglass, he took a long drink, forced the liquid past the knot in his throat and risked another glance at her expectant expression.

"It's a good idea," he admitted, and one he hadn't considered before. She was right. To put *Honor* in a class by itself, separate it from its competition, they had to point out that this movie wasn't just Hollywood doing its magic. This was life.

At its most difficult.

At its most triumphant.

She smiled at him, clearly pleased.

And Dev felt the walls around his heart trembling.

Is this what Charles had felt those long years ago? Is this what his parents had once had?

It felt as though Dev's brain was racing in circles. As Val leaned in closer to him, though, wrapping one arm around his middle, his mind shut down. No thought necessary for what he wanted now. What he *needed* now.

"Do you want dinner?" she asked, tilting her head up to kiss the underside of his jaw.

Instantly, heat swamped him and with his body hard and ready, food was the absolute last thing on his mind. He was willing to bet she knew that, too. Damn, she was good.

"Not really hungry for scallops at the moment," he said, shifting so that he could wrap his arms around her, slide his hands over the incredibly soft, silky material covering her lush body.

"Good," she said smiling. "Neither am I."

Staring down into her eyes, Dev watched as passion ignited in those violet pools. He reached for the hem of her dress, slid one hand beneath the material and up the length of her thigh.

She sighed and turned in his arms, offering herself up for his touch.

He moved his hand up, up, to the curve of her behind and then he stilled. Heartbeat thundering in his ears, he fought for breath and said, "No underwear?"

She gave a half shrug. "It would have ruined the lines of the dress."

"Let's hear it for fashion then," he muttered and took her mouth in a hungry kiss designed to send them both careening into the blaze already engulfing them.

His last coherent thought as he lost himself in her was that he was a walking dead man. His wife had somehow snapped a trap shut around him and God help him, he didn't even *want* to escape.

Seven

A week later, Dev was no closer to figuring out how he'd lost control of the situation between him and Val.

Oh, it wasn't a total loss, of course. During the day, he managed to retreat behind his wall of control enough that he felt as though he had some semblance of power. But at night, the rules changed. In their home, in their bed, Valerie was a siren he couldn't resist.

The woman he'd once considered to be too shy and timid to ever capture his attention was slowly but surely driving him to distraction. And he couldn't figure out why.

There had to be a reason behind her transformation.

She had to have some sort of scheme in mind.

All he had to do was figure out what it was.

The problem in that was that he had too much work

to do to spend enough time trying to decipher the reasons behind Valerie's complete turnaround.

But at least he had the satisfaction of knowing that at work he was in charge. In control. At the office he knew where he stood. Knew what was expected of him. Knew what to demand from everyone around him.

At home, things were different.

It wasn't just his wife that was new and improved. She'd made so many changes around his house, he could hardly keep up with them all.

In the last few days alone, he'd arrived home to find new furniture in the living room, a new bed in his bedroom and a new stove in the small kitchen he'd hardly used before bringing Val back where she belonged.

Now, not only was she cooking nearly every night, she had him *helping* her. Val had him making dinner with her every night. He was slicing onions, marinating steaks… and he was *enjoying* all of it. Not just the cooking, but spending time with her, listening to her laughter, watching her eyes shine when she was having fun.

Shaking his head, he turned his back on his office, on the stacks of correspondence and financial papers he still had to deal with, and stared instead out the windows at the bustling studio going about its business.

Not many people could see what he did at work every day. Extras walked around in full costume, everything from the carolers working on *The Christmas Wish* to what looked like a space alien sucking down a trendy coffee drink through a straw so he wouldn't mess up his dripping fangs.

It was a weird world Dev lived in and he loved it. Knew it. Appreciated it for what it was.

It was his home life that had him half crazed.

"That's a hell of a thing," he muttered, still not quite sure how she'd managed to turn his whole damn life upside down over the course of one short week.

Shaking his head, he let his mind wander back over the last several days. He found himself hurrying home from work now rather than looking for an excuse to stay late at the office. And every time he walked through the doors of their suite, he found something new waiting for him.

Hell, he hardly recognized his own place now, what with all the overstuffed furniture and throw pillows and brightly colored rugs she had scattered all over the floors. There were flowers in vases, music was always playing and the whole damn place smelled like her perfume.

But she'd changed more than his house, Dev thought, she'd changed *him* and he wasn't entirely sure he was comfortable with that.

What he had to do was retake control of the situation. Stop being so passive about all this. Remind her just who the hell he was. No more letting Valerie make all the moves, set up all the surprises.

If he wanted this marriage to work out the way he'd planned—and he did—then he needed to be the one calling the shots.

He was going to stop being dragged around by desire. No matter how much he was enjoying it.

"Hey, Boss?"

He tossed a glance over his shoulder as the door to his office opened. "What is it, Megan?"

"Your wife's here."

"What?"

One of Megan's eyebrows rose, "You know? Your *wife?*"

"Funny. What the hell is Val doing here?" He came around the edge of his desk and wondered if just thinking about the woman could conjure her up. She'd never been to the studio before. But then, she was big into surprises these days, wasn't she?

Val slipped into the office, smiled at Megan and said, "Thanks. I won't keep him long. I promise."

"Oh, you keep him just as long as you like, honey."

Megan closed the door behind her. Val locked it, which had Dev wondering what she was up to and then she laughed. "Well, your assistant's just how I pictured her from your description."

His gaze locked on the upturned corner of her mouth and he felt his body fist in need. He didn't want to be glad to see her, but he was. He didn't want to remember that the door was now locked, but he did. To hide those truths from her—and from himself—Dev spoke more sharply than he'd intended. "What're you doing here, Val?"

She blinked at him. Seemed he could surprise her after all. Well, what did she expect? he wondered. Open arms? A happy little late-morning tryst on his desk? He muffled a groan as that thought settled in his brain and took root. It was all he could do not to go to her, grab her up and have her. Here.

Now.

Damn, he was as horny as a teenager with his first crush. All he could think about was sex and looking at Val now wasn't helping the situation any.

Dev couldn't take his gaze off her. She was wearing a sleek gray suit with a skirt that hit her knees, but had a slit up the side of her right thigh. Her tight gray jacket was worn over a white blouse with a deep V neckline and the sky-high heels she wore were black, to match the bag she had tucked under her arm. Her hair looked windblown, her violet eyes were shining and her mouth looked ready to be kissed.

So he didn't.

"Well," she said softly, "aren't you the crabby one?"

"Not crabby," he countered stiffly. "Busy."

This was his office. Here, he made the rules. Here, he was in charge. Completely. Home and office didn't mix. She might as well find that out now.

"What's up, Val?" He kept his voice cool deliberately.

She tipped her head to one side and a gold earring winked at him. "Is there a problem?"

"No problem," he said, walking back to his desk and sitting down behind it. He'd use the broad expanse of solid walnut like a shield. Maybe it would be enough to keep him from stripping her down and doing what he really wanted to do at the moment. "Just busy, like I said, that's all. Something you needed?"

Her expression was a blend of hurt and confusion, but he steeled himself against any guilt that might be trying to wrap itself around him. He hadn't invited her to the studio. And maybe it was time she found out that not all her surprises were going to be welcome.

"Nothing very important," she said.

"In that case…" He waved one hand at the stacks of papers in front of him.

"I did want to show you this, though," she said and opened her purse as she walked across the room toward him.

Carefully, Dev kept his gaze fixed on hers, refusing to notice how great her legs looked or how the soft gray of her jacket made her eyes look even more purple than usual. Damn it.

"What?" He leaned back in his chair, folded his hands across his abdomen, and looked up at her.

"Here, see for yourself." She handed him a sheet of paper.

It only took a moment to scan what it said, then he looked up at her again. "Not important?" he asked, using the words she had only a moment ago. "Your father's holding the center page of every one of his papers for three straight weeks for the ads we want to run for *Honor?*"

She smiled, looking pretty damn pleased with herself. "That's right. Daddy was happy to do it."

Well, hell, Dev thought as he glanced down at the handwritten note from Val's father. This was one of the main reasons Devlin had wanted to marry Valerie in the first place. The Shelton newspaper dynasty had tentacles that spread across the entire nation. With promotional material in the Shelton papers, Dev could guarantee that the ads for *Honor* would be seen by millions. It was a hell of a thing.

His publicity department would be doing backflips over this. With every studio in Hollywood out to arrange promotional space in the media, this was a gift from the heavens. Or more precisely, from his wife.

What was she up to?

"Whose idea was this?" he asked. "Your dad just suddenly decided to be generous?"

Val set her purse down onto his desk, shrugged, then

walked around his office, looking at the posters on the walls, the plaques and certificates displayed in a glass case and the magazines stacked messily on one corner of a table. Bending down, she straightened them and Dev felt a tightness in his chest as his gaze locked on the firm, round curve of her behind.

The woman was making him nuts.

Was she trying to tempt him? Or was she just doing to his office what she'd done to his home? What was next? Redecorating the place?

But the moment that thought hit him, he called himself a fool. Straightening some magazines hardly qualified as taking over.

"It was my idea," she said, glancing at him over her shoulder. "I told Daddy that I thought it would be good business for him *and* for Hudson Pictures to show a united front. You know, one big happy family?"

The very reason he'd convinced Val to give their marriage another shot, he reminded himself. Coincidence? Hell, who knew? The important thing here was, she'd arranged for publicity space with no fuss at all.

"It was a good idea," he said grudgingly.

She straightened up, slowly walked to his desk and, setting both hands on the edge, leaned into him. "Thanks." Her smile was quick, and beautiful. "How about you take me to lunch to thank me properly?"

Or, he thought, his gaze dropping to the creamy valley of skin between her breasts, he could just take her right here. On the desk. Right now. His body was hard and tight and hot, despite his every effort to keep a tight rein on the reactions she inevitably stirred in him.

She licked her lips and Dev smothered a groan. The

woman was tying him up in knots and the hell of it was, she was doing it so effortlessly.

"I don't think so," he told her, before he could change his mind. "I've got a meeting in an hour, and there's plenty of paperwork to catch up on before then."

"Oh." She sounded disappointed.

Well, hell. So was he. But he had to draw a line somewhere, didn't he? "Come on. I'll walk you to your car."

He stood up and came around the desk. He took her hand and she instantly wrapped her fingers around his and squeezed. She looked up at him through her lashes and said, "How about a quick tour of the studio before I leave then? I've never really seen this place before and I'd like to know more about what you do."

Dev stood there, hot and eager for her, and when she moved the tips of her fingers against his palm, everything in him went even harder than it had been a moment ago.

Voice tight and low with a need that was just barely being kept in check, he asked, "Val, what're you doing? Why're you really here?" His hand on hers tightened, stilling the touch of her fingers. "You could have given me that note from your father at home. So why come here?"

"I just wanted to see you," she said, her voice a caressing whisper of sound. "Is that so hard to believe?" She moved in closer and laid one hand over his heart. When she felt the rapid slam of it against her palm, she added, "I wanted to find out if you missed me as much as I miss you during the day."

He groaned, let his head fall back, then straightened again to stare down at her. "This isn't the time," he said and each word sounded as if it had cost him a terrible price to utter. "Isn't the place."

"Why not?"

She had a point. Why the hell not?

She smiled again. "The door's locked. We're here. Alone. And I want you, Dev. So much."

Screw control. A man could only hold out for so long, he told himself as he grabbed her, yanked her in close and took her mouth in a hard, frantic kiss. Her tongue met his in a clash of desperate need and Dev knew this battle was lost. He had to have her. Now. This minute. He didn't care if half the studio was waiting for him outside his door. All he cared about was here in this room.

Val slipped her arms around his neck and held on. She had her answer. He did miss her. He did think about her while they were apart. And her coming here to the office, imprinting herself on his brain while he was at work, had been the best idea she'd had yet. Now he wouldn't be able to put her out of his mind even when he was locked away working.

Her mouth fused to his, she tasted his heat, swallowed his breath and gave him hers. Every inch of her body was humming wildly with need, with passion that seemed never to be quieted. It didn't matter how many times they came together. She always wanted more. Always wanted *him*.

He tore his mouth from hers, buried his face in the curve of her neck and nibbled at the base of her throat. How was it possible that he could make her feel so much? How had she managed to *not* feel this the first time they had come together?

She'd reentered her marriage with the notion of seducing Dev and holding him to her with the silky strands of sexual heat. But she hadn't expected to like sex this much herself. Every time he touched her, she felt something new. Something more vital. Something more compelling.

Val fought for air as electricity seemed to explode inside her. Her body was hot and wet and so ready for him she thought if he didn't take her that moment, she might fragment into a million jagged pieces from the stress of wanting so deeply.

Then his hands were at her waist and he was turning her around to face the desk. "Dev?"

"Bend forward," he ordered, "and hold on to the desk."

Instinctively, she did as he said, her gaze locked on the scene beyond the windows. Only then did she realize that the entire world could be watching them. It was one thing to seduce her husband. It was another to perform for an audience. "Dev. Quick. Shut the blinds."

"No need," he told her, his voice a rough rasp of sound. "The windows are tinted. No one can see in."

At those words, a swirl of something wickedly exciting lit up inside Val as she felt Dev's hands at the hem of her skirt. Outside this office, the world went on. She could see them, but they had no idea what was happening right in front of them. And somehow, that knowledge made what was happening between her and Dev that much more thrilling.

Slowly, he slid the material up her legs, inch by luscious inch. She wiggled in place at the touch of his fingers against her heated skin. The cool air of the room brushed over her bare thighs and her own internal heat spiked in response. This was magic, she told herself, biting down on her bottom lip as she reminded herself to breathe.

She heard him open the zipper of his slacks and then her skirt was hiked all the way to her waist. She knew he was seeing the dark red lace thong she'd worn for his benefit, just in case. And she wondered what his expression was like. But she didn't want to look. She wanted only to feel. To stare out that window at an unsuspecting world and let Dev take her to the heights only he could.

"Beautiful," he whispered, and she felt him bend over her. Then his lips and teeth worked at the sensitive flesh at the small of her back and she groaned softly, moving against him, into him.

"But," he added, snapping the fragile elastic of her panties and pulling them off her, "we're going to have to get these out of the way."

"Dev…"

"Shh…" he whispered and fitted his palms to the curve of her bottom. Long, strong fingers massaged her skin and she tightened her grip on the edge of the desk, hoping she wouldn't fall over and ruin this spectacular moment.

"Open your blouse," he said, his tone brooking no argument.

Wobbly, a little off-balance, she did as he wanted, quickly undoing the tiny buttons that lined the front of her tidy white blouse. The lace of her bra felt unbearably scratchy against her sensitive skin and when Devlin reached one hand around her to cup one breast in his palm, she actually whimpered at the contact. His thumb and forefinger played with her nipple through the fragile material of her bra and the sensations were incredible.

"Devlin," she whispered and heard the break in her voice, "please…"

He pulled her hair away from her neck and nibbled at her skin as he shifted his free hand from her breast to the aching center of her need. Instantly, heat exploded within her and she nearly purred with contentment as he stroked her intimately with the tips of his fingers. She widened her stance, giving him access, silently asking him to touch her more deeply, more fully. To enter her and end the sweet torment he was causing.

But he was clearly in no rush to end this encounter. Again and again, he touched her, smoothing over her swollen folds, teasing the tiny bud at the core of her, making her want more and more until her body vibrated with a pulsing hunger that hammered at her for release.

"Now, Devlin. Please, *now.*"

"Yes," he said on a groan. "Now."

He thrust deep, one swift stroke from behind that had Val gasping for air. She bent over farther, pushing back against him, wanting to feel him even deeper inside. His neatly stacked papers were knocked from the desk and neither of them noticed. He rocked his hips against her, caressed her backside and slid his hands up and down her spine as he took her over and over again, pushing her higher, racing with her toward the precipice that waited just out of reach.

Val's vision blurred and the scene beyond the windows became nothing more than a wild blend of colors and movement. All she felt, all she cared about was what Dev was doing to her. His body pressed into hers, his body claiming hers, his hot breath on her neck as he leaned over her, whispering erotic, wicked suggestions as he laid siege to her body with hot, hard thrusts.

And when she felt as though she couldn't stand any more pleasure without shattering, the end grabbed her and held on. She bit down hard on her bottom lip to keep from screaming out his name as wave after wave of pulsing satisfaction rippled through her. Before the last of those tremors died away, she felt him tense and then heard his groan as a moment later, his body emptied itself into hers.

As he groaned her name, his arm came around her middle and held her tightly to him, as though he was cushioning her fall from a truly dizzying height.

Moments—maybe *hours* later, who knew for sure?—Val heard Devlin ask, "Are you okay?"

"I'm way better than okay," she assured him and almost protested when he withdrew from her body and carefully tugged her skirt into place.

Slowly, she straightened up and leaned one hip against the desk to keep from toppling over. Her knees were weak and it felt as if every muscle in her body had gone as limp as cooked spaghetti.

She looked at Dev and watched as he closed up his slacks. He looked as shaken as she felt, and that was good, Val thought. She'd hate to be the only one reacting to whatever it was that lay between them.

Buttoning up her blouse, Val kept her gaze locked with his and smiled. "That was much nicer than lunch."

"Yeah," Dev said, but he scowled rather than smiled as he said it. "Yeah, it was."

"Your frown really sells that," she told him, tipping her head to one side and studying him carefully. She knew he'd felt what she had. She'd experienced his hunger, his release almost as completely as she had her own. So why would he retreat now? Why would he pull away even though they were standing right beside each other?

"Sorry," he muttered, moving around her to gather up the papers they'd pushed off the desk. He set them down in a neat pile again, bent down to pick up her discarded panties and tucked them into his pocket before he turned to face her. Reaching out, he cupped the back of her neck, pulled her in for a fast, hard kiss and then gave her a forced smile that didn't come close to reaching his eyes. "It was great. Really. But I *do* have that meeting coming up and—"

"Fine." Val cut him off and took a breath. She'd known going in that this was going to take some time. Winning her husband, making him fall in love with her, wasn't going to happen overnight. So there was no point in becoming disappointed or in letting him see that she was discouraged by the way he could shut himself off so completely.

"Maybe you could come back next week? I'll give you that tour of the studio and we can have lunch at the commissary."

It was her turn to plaster a less-than-sincere smile on her face, so Valerie did just that. "I'd like that. And maybe we could do this again, too…" She stroked the edge of his desk with her fingertip.

His blue eyes flashed and Valerie felt better. He might be able to pretend that what they shared meant nothing more than a good orgasm. But there was more. She knew it. All she had to do was make him believe it.

He cleared his throat, grabbed his suit jacket off the

back of his desk chair and slipped it on. Then he came around his desk, took her hand in his and said, "Come on. This time I *will* walk you to your car."

When he unlocked the office door, he said, "I'll be back in a few minutes, Megan."

As he led her across the reception area, Valerie caught Megan Carey's eye and grinned when the older woman gave her a wink and a thumb's up.

Seemed she had allies.

She also, Val told herself an hour later, had a few enemies.

"Come on, Valerie. One statement for our readers."

She'd stopped at an organic grocery store on Melrose to pick up a few things and now, Valerie was regretting the impulse. After a little afternoon loving with her husband, the last thing she wanted to do was face down a reporter.

Especially this one.

Carrie Soker, a too-tall, too-thin, gossip tabloid reporter had been sitting on the hood of Val's car waiting for her and clearly had no intention of getting off the car until she got her quote. The overhead sun threw Carrie's face into shadow and seemed to define its sharp planes harshly.

"Carrie," Val asked in a tired, oh-so-patient voice, "don't you ever get tired of Hudson hunting?"

The woman had the nerve to grin. Not a good look. Her face was skeletally thin. She wore dark red lipstick, green eye shadow on the lids of her brown eyes, and had her brown hair pulled back from her face with an alligator clip. She wore blue jeans, a black, long-sleeved

T-shirt and running shoes—no doubt so she could chase her quarry down if they tried to escape.

"Why would I get tired of it?" she asked. "There are so many of you that there's always variety."

"Good," Val told her, loading her groceries from the cart into the trunk of her small SUV. "Go find variety. Go bother someone else. Luc. Or Max."

"Please. Luc's in Montana and Max is on studio grounds," Carrie snapped with a frown. "I can't get past the guard. Yet, anyway."

Finished unloading her purchases, Val slammed the trunk shut, pushed the cart out of the way, then walked to the driver's side door, glaring at Carrie, still perched cozily on her hood. "What is it you want?"

"I'm just trying to make a living, you know?" Carrie laid one hand against her chest and tried to look innocent. It was as convincing as a barracuda masquerading as a goldfish. "You Hudsons are news, you know? And now that you and Devlin seem to have patched everything up, you're even bigger news."

"Our marriage is our business," Val said.

"That's where you're wrong." Carrie scooted off the hood, took two steps and stopped on the other side of the driver's side door that Val had opened and slipped behind. "You're news. All of you. Hell, your own father's a newspaperman. You know how this works."

"Yes," Val pointed out, "but my father's papers don't report on aliens driving school buses."

Carrie grinned again and wiggled two straggly brown brows. "That wasn't my piece, but it was a good one. Now, how about you give me a good quote that we can run tomorrow?"

"Fine, here's one."

"Excellent." Carrie hit her tape-recorder button, held it out and waited.

"Valerie Hudson claimed to have no comment when pestered by annoying reporter."

Carrie scowled at her and shut the recorder off. "Real funny. But you know I'm not going away, right?"

"Just like death and taxes," Val muttered, sliding into her car. She tried to close the door, but Carrie grabbed it first.

"Just answer me this. Did you and Devlin get back together just for the Oscars? Want to make everything look happy and rosy before the big night?"

Val flushed. Instantly, the memory of Devlin saying almost those exact words the day he'd come to bring her home filled her mind. But that wasn't the only reason, was it? No. She knew he felt more for her now than he had then. He couldn't be faking his responses to her. The passion. The hunger...

"Oooh," Carrie murmured with a cagey smile, "looks like I hit a nerve."

Valerie shook her head, cleared her mind and focused on the woman staring at her with shark's eyes. "What you *hit*," she said coolly, "is the end of my patience. Go bother someone else, all right?"

Then she jerked the car door free of the woman's greedy fingers and slammed it closed. Firing up the engine, she put the car in reverse, turned to look behind her and bulleted out of the parking place. She drove away without looking back, so Val missed seeing Carrie Soker doing a happy little dance in place.

Eight

"Next time you talk to that damned woman, tell me about it. I don't *like* surprises," Dev shouted the next morning.

"All I told her was to go away."

"You shouldn't have talked to her at all." Devlin waved the paper in one tight fist and squeezed as if he could make the damn thing disappear with a little effort.

"It wasn't as if I could avoid her," Val pointed out in her own defense. "The woman was planted on my car like a hood ornament."

"Next time, run her over. It'll be easier to deal with." Dev's gaze dropped to the headline of the trashy grocery-store rag he'd picked up when he went out for muffins and coffee.

Another Hudson Marriage in Trouble? His blood

boiled as he looked at the computer-generated image of him and Val facing away from each other. And underneath those bold black letters and the picture was, Devlin and Valerie Together for the Sake of Oscar. True Love Not in Hudson's cards.

"She's making it up," Val told him for the fifth time.

"Of course she's making it up," Dev ranted and tossed the damn paper down onto the closest table. "That's not the point. By talking to her, you've given her an edge toward believability."

"So this is all my fault?" Val came up out of her chair and stalked across the room to grab up the paper he'd tossed down.

And even through his frustrated fury, a part of Dev was watching his wife and admiring the fire in her. If asked, he'd have had to say he much preferred this new Val to the one he'd known months ago.

Then she was yelling at him and he decided it'd be safer to pay attention.

"Some crazy woman stalks me, I tell her to get lost and I'm the bad guy because she writes some delusional article for this piece of trash paper she works for?"

"You're right. I know you're right. I'm just…so pissed I can't see straight."

"Fine. Be mad. At *her.*"

Frustrated and irritated beyond belief, Devlin shoved one hand through his hair and stalked across the room to the fireplace. Setting both hands on the mantel, he stared into the mirror above the hearth and looked at his wife watching him.

It was Sunday morning. He'd planned on spending

it leisurely exploring his wife's luscious curves, delighting both of them with new and inventive methods of making love. And if he hadn't volunteered to go out for coffee and muffins, that's exactly what they'd be doing at the moment.

But no. Now he had to worry about that idiot reporter slamming his family. Again.

"This isn't about just us, is it?" Val asked, her voice quieter, her expression thoughtful.

He kept his gaze locked on her reflection as he shook his head. "No. Read it. You'll see she spares plenty of room to toast my parents' breakup and to bring up the scandal about Bella again."

He waited while she read the short, vicious article, then when she lifted her gaze to look at him, Dev turned around to face her.

"I'm sorry about that, Dev, but honestly, I didn't tell her anything."

Disgusted with himself, he blew out a breath. "I know that. It's just, Bella's past the hurt now. She's got Sam and she's happy. And my parents' business is just that—their business. I hate seeing it all played out in the paper again."

She folded the gossip sheet and tossed it to the floor before walking toward him. Her soft blue robe was belted loosely at her waist and he caught tantalizing glimpses of her bare legs as she came toward him.

When she was no more than an arm's reach from him, she stopped, lifted one hand and cupped his cheek. Giving him a wry smile, she said, "If it helps, Carrie's story on us is running right beneath the article on a woman in Colorado who's in contact with Saturn."

He snorted a laugh.

She smiled. "No one's going to pay any attention to it, Dev. No one who matters, anyway."

"I suppose."

"And we know that the Oscars wasn't the only reason you came to get me, don't we?" She looked up into his eyes and waited for his response.

The Academy Awards was the reason he'd given himself for going to her. But even then, he'd known it wasn't the whole truth. And now? Now he wanted her here too much. He admired her almost as much as he desired her. It worried him just how much she was coming to mean to him. But he wouldn't love her. He'd never let it go that far. Because if he let her in too deeply, he'd be giving her the very ammunition she needed to devastate him.

But he couldn't tell her any of that, so he smiled instead and reached for her. Wrapping his arms around her, he tucked his face into the curve of her neck and whispered, "Yeah, baby. We know the truth."

"So what is the truth?"

"Good question," Dev muttered and leaned back in his desk chair. He spun the thing around so he could watch the activity on the back lot while he talked to his younger brother Luc on the phone.

He'd told Luc all about the article Carrie Soker had written and about the argument he and Val had had over it the day before. "Val says she didn't talk to Carrie and she probably didn't. But the fact is, she did see the reporter and didn't bother to mention it until I saw the damned article in the paper myself. Why wouldn't she tell me? Why keep that a secret?"

"Maybe she didn't think it was important enough to mention," Luc suggested. "After all, the Hudsons have been hounded into the ground by reporters for years. Hell, I chased Leslie Shay off the ranch last week. And good ol' Leslie bothered Gwen, too."

But Dev was focused on the fact that Val hadn't even mentioned the confrontation to him. "She's always asking me about *my* day, why the hell didn't she tell me about hers?"

"Are you actually *looking* for problems?"

"Don't have to look," Dev muttered. "I opened my eyes and there they are."

"Damn, Dev," Luc said, his voice sounding as strong as though he were in the same room, not out on the Montana ranch he shared with his wife, Gwen, and their son, Chaz. "Haven't you wised up yet?"

Dev lifted his legs to the windowsill and crossed his feet at the ankles. "What do you mean?"

"I mean, Val's not the enemy. She's not out to submarine you. She's your wife."

"I know who the hell she is."

"Yeah, but you don't act like it."

"Excuse me?" Dev frowned as though his younger brother could see the expression. "You're in Montana, for God's sake, how do you know how I'm acting?"

"Because, I know *you*," Luc said with a laugh. "You've always been the one to back off anytime somebody got close."

"Look who's talking," Dev told him. "I didn't see you and Gwen having a happy, shiny time of it."

There was a long pause, then Luc muttered, "That's different."

"Yeah, because it's you. Well, this is me and I can handle my own life, thanks."

"Sure," Luc muttered. "Because you've done a bang-up job so far."

"Did you call just to give me a headache?" Devlin frowned again and watched as a space alien and an eighteenth-century woman walked hand in hand toward the commissary.

"No, that's just a bonus," Luc admitted, laughing. "I'm actually calling to tell you Gwen and I will be there for Oscar night."

"That's great, Luc." He smiled to himself. The whole family together. That's what they needed. To show Hollywood, to show the world, that the Hudsons were a unit that wouldn't be divided.

Of course, as soon as that thought registered, he remembered that his parents were still separated and that he had no cure for his mother's betrayal or his father's pain. And he was no closer to trusting the woman who was his wife. How the hell could he? She'd already left him once. Why would he let himself care only to watch her walk out again? What would be the point?

"Dad'll be pleased," Dev said.

"And Mom?" Luc said softly.

"Don't."

"She's our mother, damn it."

"I know that. You think this is easy on me?" Dev asked.

"I think you're making it harder than it has to be," Luc said. "What happened with Mom was so long ago...."

"Yeah, but it's here now, isn't it?" Dev felt a stab of pain in the middle of his chest. The anger at his mother was mostly gone, but the sense of betrayal was something he couldn't get past. "Look at what happened to Bella because of it."

"Bella's putting it behind her. Maybe you should think about trying it, too."

"Let it go, Luc." Dev didn't want to talk about this with Luc, with anyone. The sting of his mother's betrayal still resonated too deeply with him. And he wasn't going to "get past it" by talking it over with his siblings.

"Fine," Luc said after a long, silent moment. "You always were the most stubborn of us. So why don't you just tell me what's going on at the studio."

Grateful for the shift in subject, Devlin shook his thoughts away and concentrated on the sound of his brother's voice. "Regretting your decision to move and become a full-time cowboy?"

"Hell no," Luc said with a laugh. "I just want to hear how crazy you Hollywood types are. Remind me how good I have it out here."

Dev was happy for his brother. Hell, for all his siblings. They'd all managed to find that one person who seemed to complete them. If he resented the fact that his life was less settled than the rest of them, well, that would just continue to be his little secret. He was the oldest. It was up to him to make sure the family stayed strong. And if ensuring that meant keeping his wife at a safe distance from his heart, then that's what he'd do.

The ties holding the Hudson family together were already being tested, thanks to what had happened between his parents. He wouldn't add to the stress by trusting his heart to the wrong woman only to have her smash it.

"Fine, let me tell you what Max is up to first. He's always the most entertaining," Dev said and settled in for a long talk with his brother.

Malibu was more than a beach. It was Hollywood West.
Years ago, this stretch of sand had been crowded with tidy bungalows, cottages used by owners who came out on summer weekends. Now those cottages were mostly gone, replaced by mini-mansions that hugged the shore and were threatened by high tides almost annually.
Now, at the end of February, the ocean was slate gray, reflecting the cloud cover overhead and only a few hardy surfers dared the frigid water. The wind was cold and harsh, the beach mostly empty and the cries of the seagulls wheeling in the air sounded like screams.
Val loved it. She loved standing at the edge of Jack Hudson's property with the laughter and shouts of the Hudsons behind her and the great sweep of sand and sea in front of her. The back of Jack's house was mainly glass, allowing them an unobstructed view of the water, while cliffs behind the house were filled with brush and a few twisted cypress trees. At the shore's edge, a black lab raced through the frothy water chasing a stick thrown by its owner.
Still smiling, she turned to look at the group crowded together on Jack Hudson's patio. The whole Hudson family—save for Luc and Gwen who were in Montana, and Jack's sister, Charlotte, and her husband, who were at their home in France—were gathered here for a barbecue. Even Sabrina and Markus had both attended, though Val hadn't seen them speak to each other yet. Despite that bit of tension, the day was going well.

Almost three-year-old Theo Hudson was giggling on his grandmother's lap as Sabrina tickled and teased him. The adults were gathered around the smoking barbecue or lounging on the deck chairs scattered across the wide patio. Another burst of laughter rose into the air and Val sighed in response.

This was one of the things she'd dreamed of when she had married Dev. This whole loud, confusing, wonderful gathering of an extended family. As the only child of a workaholic widower, Val had never really been a part of anything like this before. And she meant to make the most of it.

She pushed wind-blown hair out of her eyes as her gaze quite naturally slid across the crowd until she found Dev. In his worn blue jeans, black T-shirt and dark green sweater, he looked more like an adventurer than an executive. And she realized she liked him in both of his personas. Though this Dev seemed more approachable. More relaxed somehow.

"Don't look now, but you're drooling."

"What?" Val jumped, startled and turned to look at her sister-in-law. Shaking her head, she demanded, "Bella. Are you *trying* to scare me to death?"

"No," the other woman said with a smile. "Sorry. I was just noticing how you were noticing Dev."

"Obvious again?" Just what she needed, Val thought. She knew that every one of the Hudson family had been very aware before how crazy she was about Dev and how little he'd returned that affection. She so didn't want to go through that again.

"I know what you're thinking," Bella told her and leaned back against the weathered red fence surrounding Jack's property. "But you're wrong. Nobody thought less of you back then, Val. We were all mad at Devlin."

"Oh, thanks," she said wryly. "That makes it all better."

"I'm just saying, we were on your side then and we're on your side now."

"What happened to Hudson solidarity?" She glanced at Bella then shifted her gaze back to where Dev stood talking to his brother Max. Seriously, how did one family produce so many gorgeous men?

"Oh, there's solidarity all right. We're solidly behind *you*." Bella dropped one arm around her shoulders and said, "I told you, you're the best thing that ever happened to Dev. And I'm not the only one here who thinks so."

As good as it made her feel to know that her husband's family were being supportive, it didn't matter to her as much as what Dev was thinking. "Thanks, but it only matters if *Dev* thinks so."

"He does." Bella gave her a squeeze, then let go. "But he's a man, honey. They learn slow."

"I hope that's all it is," Val said a little wistfully. Nothing had really changed between her and Dev.

They'd been back together more than two weeks and she was no closer to breaking down his emotional walls than she had been the first night she'd seduced him.

Oh, the sex was amazing. At night, when they were locked together, she felt closer to him than to anyone she'd ever known and she knew that he felt the same thing. But once the sun was up, everything shifted again, with Devlin becoming more remote, more the man she remembered from the first time she'd tried to build a marriage all by herself.

Why was he so determined to keep her at arm's length? Why wouldn't he let her in? Didn't he know that they couldn't go on this way forever? Frowning, Val watched her husband scowl at Max and felt something give her heart a hard squeeze. As much as she loved him, she wouldn't settle for being his partner only in the darkness. She wanted all of him. And this time, she wasn't going to settle for less.

"Did you talk to Mom?" Max asked as he handed Dev another beer.

"No." Dev's gaze slid to where Sabrina Hudson sat on a deck chair, Theo on her lap. She was still a beautiful woman, he thought, though for the first time, he noticed a strain of unhappiness around her eyes. "Not yet."

"I'm glad she came. I know it meant a lot to Cece and Jack to have her and Dad here."

Dev took a long drink of his beer. "Yeah, but did they ask Dad how *he'd* feel about it?"

"Why would they?" Max frowned at him. "This is a family thing. Everyone's invited, you know that. Besides, does it look like Dad minds?"

Dev followed Max's pointing finger to find his father, seated not far from his wife, watching her through shadowed eyes. Despite the whirl of laughter and conversation surrounding them, Markus and Sabrina looked to be on their own private, hellish islands. He could almost feel his father's pain from there.

"He doesn't look happy."

"Neither does Mom," Max pointed out.

"And whose fault is that?" Dev snapped.

"Damn, Dev." Max shook his head and stared at him. "Are you really so perfect you can't forgive anyone else for being human? You're wasting your time running a movie studio. You should be a saint."

"Didn't say I was perfect," Dev muttered darkly and took another swallow of icy cold beer.

"Yeah? It's how you act. What? Nobody makes mistakes in your little world?"

He stiffened, glared at his younger brother and shifted another look across the patio at his mother, still holding a squirming Theo on her lap. As he watched, his mother raised her chin to smile at Dana, then accepted a glass of iced tea that she shared with little Theo.

And just watching her made Dev realize that he'd really missed having his mother around the mansion. Sabrina had always been the one to laugh the loudest and love the hardest. Hell, he could remember dozens of times when he was a kid that he had gone without seeing his father—busy at the studio. But Sabrina had always been there for her children.

Funny, he hadn't thought of that in a long time.

Shaking his head, he took another drink of his beer and said, as much for his own benefit as for Max's, "Sure, people make mistakes, but then they've got to pay for them."

"With what?" his brother demanded, moving to block Dev's view of his mother. "A public flogging?"

"Don't be stupid."

"I'm not the idiot in this conversation," Max told him. "You keep holding Mom's mistakes against her, but how about looking at it from her side?"

"What *is* her side then, Mister Tuned In To His Feminine Side?"

Max scowled at him. "How about a mistake she made thirty years ago came back to bite her publicly? How about her daughter was tortured by the press? Her marriage was dissected in sound bytes? How about her own damn oldest son won't talk to her and give her a chance to tell him what she's feeling?"

Irritated, Dev shifted uncomfortably. Fine. So he'd had a case of tunnel vision where this thing with his parents had been concerned. But what the hell else was he supposed to think? His mother wasn't the woman he'd thought she was and how the hell was he supposed to reconcile that now?

"Damn, you really are the most stubborn human being on the planet," Max mused. "Bella always said so, but I completely get it now."

"I'm not stubborn," Dev said, "I'm—"

"Rigid? Inflexible?" Max provided

"Consistent," Dev said uncomfortably, then added, "either change the subject or go away."

Max blew out a breath, shrugged and said, "Fine. How's this? The wedding plans are getting way out of hand."

"What?" Dev stared at his brother and waited for more of an explanation.

"It's like planning an invasion."

And Max looked more happy about that than Dev had seen him in a long time. How was it, he wondered, that what had happened to his parents' marriage didn't seem to affect how any of his siblings thought about the whole married thing? Was he the only one to be bitten by the caution bug? Didn't anyone else see the inherent risks in trusting someone so much?

"Nothing to say?" Max nudged.

"Just that you're a lucky man," Dev said and slapped his brother on the back. He was glad Max was happy again. And the whole family already liked and accepted Dana, so that was a plus. It was his own confusion that had Dev's head spinning.

"I know," Max said.

A ping of envy resonated inside Dev briefly and he almost wished he could be as unconcernedly happy as his brother. But someone in this family had to keep thinking straight, didn't they?

Dev glanced their way and noticed that his mother did look happy, though her eyes still held a shadow of pain. Guilt reared its ugly head for a moment, but Dev squashed it mercilessly.

"And," Max added, pointing with his beer bottle, "looks like Bella and Val are having a great time, too."

Dev glanced across the yard at his wife, laughing and talking quietly with his sister. He frowned.

Max said warily, "Always makes me nervous when women get together to whisper."

"Yeah," Devlin murmured. "Me, too."

He caught Val's gaze and when she smiled, his chest felt lighter, as if he'd somehow shrugged off an invisible weight he hadn't even realized he was carrying. How'd she do that? he wondered absently. How did she manage to make him feel as if he wasn't the loner he'd always been at these gatherings?

Before Val, he would watch his brothers and sisters with their dates or their mates and be the extra wheel.

The one who kept his heart locked away. The one who stayed on the fringes and watched everyone else live their lives.

Now with Val here, he felt more of a part of the festivities than he ever had. And he wondered when the hell that had happened. His gaze moved over his wife, dressed in blue jeans, tennis shoes and a long, tunic style deep lavender sweater that made her eyes look as dark and mysterious as twilight.

His body tightened and something inside him shifted, making air a little harder to come by. Frowning to himself, he worked hard to avoid his body's automatic response to Val and told himself it meant nothing. Nothing. But even he didn't believe him.

"Wonder what they're talking about," he murmured.

"Probably best if we don't know," Max told him just before he wandered off to find Dana.

"Probably," Dev whispered to himself, his gaze still locked on his wife. As Bella walked off toward Sam, Val strolled toward the crowd of Hudsons by the main table. She made her way to Sabrina, bent down and kissed the older woman's cheek in greeting. Dev saw his mother's eyes light up and for a second or two, he felt tension bleed from him. Val. She knew his family, obviously cared for them, and they felt the same, that was plain enough to see.

She fit in well with everyone, he thought and realized that Val had carved out a niche for herself in the family. Seeing her with his mother made him want to go over there himself. Maybe Max was right. Maybe there was more to all of this than he'd thought. Maybe he owed it to Sabrina to hear her out.

But even as he considered it, he knew that whatever his mother's reasons, she'd betrayed a trust and he just couldn't find a way around that. So instead, he focused on Val, though his feelings for her were just as confusing.

He'd watched her earlier, playing with Theo, laughing with his father, chatting with Jack's wife, Cece. And now, there she was, sitting on the patio beside Sabrina's chair, playing with Theo, chatting with his mom. Val fit in so seamlessly it was as if she'd always been there.

And that worried him, too. Hell, he told himself as that thought settled in, maybe he was as crazy as Luc had suggested. Maybe he was making trouble where there wasn't any. Why couldn't he just relax and enjoy his wife?

Because, he thought, taking a sip of the cold beer and lifting his face into the slap of the sea wind, it was safer to be on guard. To remember that he'd married Val for her newspaper connections. For the fact that she was intelligent and beautiful and would make an excellent hostess.

The fact that she damn near set his sheets on fire was just a bonus.

The unmistakable clink of a knife against crystal sounded out and the Hudson clan quieted for an announcement.

Jack Hudson grinned once he had everyone's attention. Then he held out one hand toward his wife and Cece slipped up next to him, wrapped her arms around his middle and smiled up at him.

Jack gave her a quick, hard kiss, then looked out at his family. "I guess you're wondering why we called you all here today...."

"To play with *me!*" Theo shouted, then dissolved into giggles as his grandmother kissed his neck.

A few laughs burst into the air at the little boy's shout, but Dev just stood there, waiting. Apparently, more than one family member had something to say today.

"Well, sure, that's part of the reason," Jack told his son, then spoke up even louder as he said, "Cece and I have an announcement." His voice carried easily over the wind and the surge of the sea. Then he paused for dramatic effect and shouted, "We're going to have another baby!"

Cheers erupted from the family as everyone there rushed to hug and congratulate Dev's cousin and his wife. Even Theo was excited, shouting something about baby brothers and puppies. But Dev hardly heard any of it.

He was too caught up in the look Valerie was sending him. It clearly said that she would love to be pregnant. To be announcing that *they* were having a baby. Devlin stilled. He felt as though time had stopped and he and Val were caught in a bubble, separate from everyone else as their locked gazes linked them together.

A *baby?*

Was he ready for that? He'd better be, he thought suddenly, since as far as he knew, they hadn't been doing anything to prevent conception. And why hadn't he thought about that before right now? A father? Him? Hell, he wasn't really ready for the wife Val had become.

Before the cheers for Jack and Cece had died away, Max was on his feet, holding on to Dana as if half expecting her to try to escape him. Then he announced,

"As long as we're all celebrating… Don't forget about our wedding!"

Another round of happy shouts and laughter rose up and as the Hudsons celebrated, Dev looked at his wife and tried to come to terms with a marriage he hadn't expected and a woman he wanted far too much.

Nine

Three days later, Val and Sabrina were lounging in the pedicure chairs while heated jets of water massaged their feet.

"This is wonderful," Sabrina whispered on a half moan. "Thank you for suggesting it, Valerie."

"My pleasure," Val assured her, leaning her head back and closing her eyes.

The spa day had been a spontaneous suggestion the day of the picnic. Despite the family's happy news, her mother-in-law had seemed so sad, so...lost, that Val had wanted desperately to somehow ease the discomfort she was feeling. So she'd suggested a day of leisure at the best day spa in Beverly Hills.

So far, she'd have to call it a resounding success.

All she needed to make it completely perfect was to

not be worried about Dev. He'd been more withdrawn than ever since the picnic and the news from Jack and Cece. Val couldn't understand why he was so determined to keep her at bay. Why he refused to allow her all the way inside. The other members of his family seemed to have no trouble connecting with those they loved. Why did Dev?

Maybe talking with his mother was the way to gather some clues.

While they sat in silence, with piped-in classical music vying with the rush and swirl of the water in the pedicure tubs, she and Sabrina sipped cold glasses of chardonnay. They'd already had manicures, facials and body wraps, with the pedicure being the finale of their pamper day.

Val sighed into the quiet, grateful that the attendants had left her and Sabrina alone to relax for a while in private. But the moment she had too much time to think, her thoughts filled with images of Dev and her heart ached because she was no closer to winning her husband's heart.

"You're thinking about him again," Sabrina whispered, head back, eyes closed.

Val looked at the older woman beside her and could only hope that when she reached her fifties, she'd be as gorgeous. Smiling, she asked, "How did you know?"

"You were far too quiet. Which means you're thinking." Sabrina gave a casual shrug. "And, since you're married to my son—a man who is legendary for being…difficult—the direction of your thoughts wasn't hard to decipher. You love him and he's making you crazy."

Val choked out a laugh. "You could say that."

"You could also use much harsher words," Sabrina said, smiling, "but he is my son and I love him, too."

"I know." Val sat up, glanced down at her buffed and polished fingernails and said softly, "And I know that Devlin is making all of this so much harder for you."

Sighing, Sabrina sat up straight, too, and looked at her. "It's not entirely his fault. The only one to blame here is me," she admitted and looked as though she wanted to cry. But a moment later, she blinked, stiffened her chin and said, "It was such a long time ago, but the echoes of what I did just won't stop."

"Can I ask—" Val stopped, thought about it and then changed her mind. Whatever had happened all those years ago between Sabrina and her brother-in-law wasn't really her business. Though a part of her thought that the long-ago affair was at the heart of her problem with Dev, how could she ask Sabrina to talk about something that was so clearly painful?

The other woman smiled sadly. "You want to know why I did it," she said softly. "Why I slept with David."

Val nodded. "I'm sorry. I shouldn't have said anything."

"Oh, don't be sorry," Sabrina said quickly, reaching over from her chair to pat Val's hand. "I'm actually grateful. Since this whole thing came out, you're the first one to actually ask me that question. No one else wants to hear about it—though how can I blame them? My poor Bella, especially."

"I saw you talking to her at the picnic last weekend," Val said quietly.

"Yes," Sabrina said. Her smile was a little wobbly, but it was there. "It wasn't easy, but I had to try. She's my daughter and I love her."

"Of course you do," Val said hotly.

Another smile from her mother-in-law. "You don't have to defend me, Val, though I thank you for the effort." She paused, looked down at the frothing water in the pedicure tub and said, "Bella's hurt, of course. And she's very protective of her father—Markus, I mean. Because no matter what else happened so long ago, Markus *is* her father. He's a kind man. A good man. He deserved better. I think," she added thoughtfully, "Bella knows that I still love him. But she also knows that I can't regret what happened because that would mean I regret her birth. Which I don't."

"I know that, too. And yes, Markus is her father. In every way that matters," Val offered. "But if it helps any, I know that Bella misses you. She loves you very much."

Sabrina sniffled, wiped a single, stray tear from the corner of her eye and gave her a smile. "Yes, it does help. I have some hope that she'll eventually forgive me and we'll find our way back to each other. Thank you for that."

"So," Val asked, reluctant to say the words, but grateful that Sabrina had given her blessing, "if you loved Markus…why did you sleep with his brother?"

Easing back into the chair again, Sabrina looked around the small, private room. Val followed her gaze, idly noting the pale pink-wallpaper, the baskets of ferns, the reading lamps and the iced bottle of wine that sat between them.

"It seems like another lifetime ago sometimes," Sabrina whispered after a long moment of silence. "Markus was so busy at the studio back then. He was hardly home. It felt as though I was a single mother most of the time," she added wistfully. "And I suppose, the reality of the situation was, I was lonely."

"Sabrina—"

"No, no sympathy, Val. I don't deserve it. Not really. I was sorry for myself, feeling neglected by my husband and worn to the bone by my very active sons." She smiled at the memories crowding her mind, though the smile didn't last very long. "David was…attentive. His wife, Ava, was always complaining of some malady or other. The woman loved a good illness," she said, almost to herself.

Val could almost see the scenes as Sabrina told her story. A young mother, alone most of the time, her busy husband so buried in work that he didn't notice the woman he loved slipping away from him.

Actually, there were too many likenesses between her story and Sabrina's for Val's taste. But for the fact that she wasn't a mother, she could really understand how left out and alone Sabrina must have felt. And she wondered if Markus had shut his wife out of his thoughts as Dev seemed to do so easily.

"It's an old, sad story," Sabrina said. "Practically a cliché. I listened to and believed David's flattery. I craved the affection that Markus was too busy to give me and I allowed myself to believe that David really wanted me. Loved me."

"He didn't?"

"No." Sabrina turned her gaze on Val then and didn't try to hide a thing as she said, "I slept with him willingly enough, but the moment the deed was done, I regretted it. I felt horribly guilty. I'd betrayed my marriage, my husband, my family. In that blinding moment of clarity, I knew I'd risked everything that was important for one instant of selfishness. I tried to explain to David that it was all a mistake, that I loved Markus and would never do something like that again."

A chill swept along Val's spine as she asked, "What did David say?"

"He laughed." Sabrina swallowed hard and her eyes went cool and distant. "He told me that he didn't love me, that now that he'd had me, he was finished with me. And that his only reason for bedding me was to get back at Markus."

"Oh, God...." Val couldn't even imagine what Sabrina had gone through. To be used so horribly. "But he didn't tell Markus."

"No, he didn't. I suppose that knowing the truth was enough for him."

"I...don't even know what to say."

Sabrina gave her a sad smile. "No reason why you should. Even I can't believe at times that I actually was so foolish. That I almost ruined my marr—"

She broke off, obviously remembering that her marriage was now crumbling under the weight of a twenty-five-year-old secret.

"Sabrina—what about Markus?" Val asked quickly, diverting her to the past so that the future wouldn't hover quite so closely. "How did you keep the truth hidden for so long? Didn't he suspect?"

Now that she'd gotten everything off her chest, Sabrina took a long, deep breath and sighed heavily. "It nearly killed me, keeping that secret. But confession would have been for my sake, not his. The truth could only have hurt him. So I accepted the secrecy as part of my punishment.

"I couldn't bear the thought of telling him. Watching his heart break. Seeing the betrayal in his eyes." She shook her head as if wiping away all the memories. "I devoted myself to him, to the boys, and when I found out I was pregnant with Bella, I took that as a sign that I was exactly where I was meant to be. Where my heart already was. That baby would be mine and Markus's.

"I never said anything to Markus, of course, which is why this is all so devastating now...." She paused, tipped her head to one side and seemed to be considering something carefully before she said, "Sometimes, though, I suspected that Markus knew. That he had somehow guessed what I'd done. He never said anything outright," she added hastily. "But after that time with David, things changed. Markus again became the man I'd loved and married. It was as if with neither of us saying a word about it, we had both decided to devote ourselves to our family. And when Bella was born, Markus couldn't have loved her more."

Another sad smile curved her mouth as her lovely eyes brimmed with tears she refused to shed. "Now, everything is such a mess."

"I understand," Val said. "I really do."

Something in her voice must have alerted Sabrina to the fact that Val understood all too clearly.

"Oh, Valerie." She reached out one hand toward her again. "Are you and Devlin having more problems?"

Now it was Val's turn to share a sad smile. "I love him so much—"

"I know you do."

"—but it's not enough," Val finished, clutching her

mother-in-law's hand tightly. "I think he...*cares* for me, but—"

"He holds himself back."

"Yes. Exactly."

Sabrina sighed. "He was always like that, you know. Too much like his father in that way. As if letting anyone get too close was a danger signal. And, since the truth of my...indiscretion broke—well, he's only closed himself off even more. I'm sorry to say that my past mistakes are probably coloring your marriage."

Val threaded her fingers through Sabrina's and held on. Two women, in love with their husbands and seeing no real hope for rebuilding their marriages. Weren't they a sad pair?

"I don't know what to do about this, Sabrina," Val confessed. "Dev is doing to me what Markus did to you so long ago. Shutting me out. Ignoring me except in the bed—" Good God, she thought, shutting up fast. She couldn't talk to Dev's *mother* about their sex life!

But Sabrina laughed, obviously delighted. "That's good to know, Val. Trust me on this, if Dev is attentive in the bedroom, then you're on his mind. It's just going to take patience. Do you have enough patience to deal with a man as stubborn as he is?"

"I thought I did," she admitted, then realized that she was more downhearted than she had thought.

"Try, Val," Sabrina urged. "He's a good man, my son. I believe he's worth the effort."

"But it's been nearly three weeks that we've been back together and he seems no closer to letting me into his heart than he ever was."

"Three weeks isn't so very long."

"No, but how long is too long? Do I stay and risk that he'll never feel for me what I want him to?" Val asked, her voice low and filled with misery. "Or do I leave while I still can and try to make myself forget him?"

"Only you can answer that, dear," Sabrina said gently. "I can only tell you that once your heart is given, you won't find happiness anywhere else. Believe me, that is the one lesson I learned."

Before Val could say anything else, the door opened and one of the spa attendants walked in, smiling. "How are you two? All ready for your pedicure pampering?"

"Yes, thank you," Sabrina said, with a smile for Val.

"Great," the tall brunette answered. "I'll just go and get Monica and we'll be right back to take care of everything."

As she left, she allowed the door to stay open, so Val and Sabrina made a silent pact to keep quiet. No more chatting about private matters while a door into the rest of the salon stood open. Hollywood gossip spread quickly enough without *inviting* it.

Voices drifted into the room and Valerie tuned them out until she heard the name *Hudson*. Then she couldn't help but listen in.

"I'm telling you," a woman on the other side of the door was saying, "it's criminal that a man like Devlin Hudson is being wasted on that nothing-much wife of his. Please. Could she do something with her hair at least?"

Val's hand reached to smooth down her hair even as Sabrina shot her a sympathetic look. "Pay no attention," she mouthed.

But Val was listening to every word.

"It'll never last," another woman answered smugly.

"They've broken up once already and they've been married what? Four months? Devlin's going to get tired of her really soon. Heck, his own father's dumped his mother."

Sabrina inhaled sharply and Val's back teeth ground together.

"Yes, but their marriage lasted thirty years."

"That's Hollywood years, honey," the other woman told her friend. "They've probably been boffing everybody in town and managing to keep it quiet."

"In this town? It's a miracle," the first woman said on a laugh. "I'll tell you what. As soon as Markus divorces his wife, I'll swoop in and claim him. You can have Devlin when Little Miss Mousy finally splits."

"Oooh. That'd be great. You know I'm reading for a part in the next Hudson picture. I could probably find a way to 'accidentally' bump into Devlin while I'm on the lot."

"If you can't," her friend said with a chuckle, "nobody can."

"That's it," Val muttered, standing up in her pedicure footbath.

"Valerie, just let it go," Sabrina advised. "I've been around long enough to know that people talk. You can't stop it. You can't do anything about it at all."

"I can stop *them*," Val said tightly and grabbed a lush pink towel to dry her feet as she stepped out of the tub. So much for a day of pampering. She'd just have to leave the spa with naked toes because once she was finished with these two women, she wouldn't want to stick around.

"Val, don't—"

She started for the door, then stopped and looked at the mother of her husband. Hadn't Sabrina suffered enough? Was she really expected to listen to vicious cats sharpening their claws on her name? No.

"No, Sabrina. I'm finished. I'm not going to be the passive little observer standing around doe-eyed while the world does whatever it likes to me. Not again."

"Oh, my…" Sabrina was already levering herself out of the pedicure chair when Val left the room, turned a corner and glared at the two women sitting in the manicure chairs.

It was some consolation to see the looks of pure shock on their nearly-identical-Hollywood-perfect faces as she stared at them. But not nearly enough.

"How dare you sit there and spout off about me and my family," Valerie started. "Who do you think you are, anyway? Do you really presume to know what goes on in a private home? Or is the word 'private' a new one for you?"

"Now just a minute," one of them said.

"No, you had your say and we heard every word."

"We?" the other woman asked with a cringe.

Sabrina appeared in the open doorway and both women groaned.

But Valerie wasn't finished. She was on a roll now and completely enjoying herself. The fact that half the salon was now listening to every word didn't matter to her. She didn't care who else was there. It was time the world listened to Valerie so she might as well start there.

"You two think you can guess what someone's marriage is like? You think you can gossip about someone and never be called on it?"

"We didn't say anything that isn't in the papers," the first woman explained.

"Really? Which paper did the word 'mousy' appear in?" Val tapped her bare foot against the floor, planted both hands on her hips and leaned in, shooting first one of the women, then the other, looks harsh enough to melt steel. "Let me tell you something, you wanna-be-starlets. I'm not mousy. My mother-in-law's marriage is just dandy and her husband doesn't need to look to someone like *you* for comfort. As for *my* marriage, you should be so lucky as to have what I have."

"Just a min—" one of them tried to interrupt.

"And as for your 'audition'?" Val said, her voice dropping to a low growl, "one word from me and the closest either of you will get to a movie role is selling tickets in the lobby."

"Look, we're really sorry, we didn't know—"

"No, you didn't *think*," Val corrected for her. "Maybe next time you will. Now why don't you both get out of here before you find out how really 'mousy' I can be."

"Good idea," one of them said, giving her friend a hard nudge. "C'mon, Dani, let's jet."

"Right behind you," her friend said as they gathered up their purses and headed for the door.

Once they were gone, a smattering of applause broke out in the salon. Val's temper was still spiking so hotly she hardly noticed.

Sabrina stepped up, wrapped her in a tight hug and said, "Brava!" Then she leaned back, looked her in the eyes and said, "I couldn't ask for a finer daughter-in-law."

Val grinned and felt a surge of triumph she'd never

known before. Who would have guessed that standing up for herself could feel so…wonderful? At the moment, she even felt as if she could face down Dev and come out the winner.

"Thanks. What do you say we blow off the pedicures and go have a late lunch?"

Devlin walked in the door, tossed his keys onto the table in the entryway and walked into the main room of his suite. He was used to the changes in his home now and actually liked them, though he hadn't told Val that. The overstuffed furniture was more comfortable than his old leather pieces and he had to say, he thought with a smile, that he definitely approved of Val's "snuggle sofa" idea.

Just remembering their first night on that couch in front of a candlelit hearth had him going hard and ready for her. Amazing just how easily he was aroused with thoughts of Valerie. Even more amazing that he was somehow able to block thoughts of her during the day only to lose himself in her once he got home.

Shaking his head, he looked around the room and when he didn't see her or hear her, called out, "Val?"

"I'm in here," she shouted back and he smiled, already headed for the kitchen.

It was quickly becoming his favorite room in the house. Who would have guessed that cooking together every night could be so much fun? Although, he had to admit that sex on the table last night had added to the allure of the room. Maybe he could talk her into a fast, sweaty bout of sex before dinner tonight, too.

He pulled off his jacket, tossed it to a chair and was

pulling his tie off as he walked into the kitchen. Val was at the butcher block table in the center of the room, slicing onions, and the smile she gave him told him that she'd be open to anything he might suggest. But first, something smelled great and he made straight for the bubbling pot on the back of the stove. "What've you got going here?"

"Spaghetti sauce."

He looked at her. "From scratch?"

She grinned and tossed her hair back out of her eyes. "Is there any other kind?"

Until Valerie had entered his life, he thought, he would have made do with jarred sauce and a table for one. Or, he would have gone down to the family dining room to eat whatever they were serving.

Shaking his head, he lifted the lid off the pot and took a deep breath of the incredible scents drifting up in a tower of steam. "Smells great."

"Tastes even better," she assured him. "Want to help slice onions?"

"It's what I live for," he told her and walked around to stand directly behind her. Laying his hands over hers, he leaned in close, making sure she could feel his body, hard and eager for her. He wanted her to know without a doubt that slicing vegetables wasn't what he had in mind.

She sucked in a gulp of air. "Dev, if you do that, I'm liable to chop both of our hands off."

"Maybe you'd better set the knife down, then."

"But dinner—"

"Not what I'm hungry for," he told her and, when she dropped the knife onto the cutting surface, turned her around in his arms. Deftly then, he undid the buttons of her blouse and just as handily unhooked the front snaps of her bra.

"This is what I need, right here," he murmured, freeing her breasts and palming their weight.

Her head fell back, her eyes closed and she sighed heavily. "That shouldn't feel so good. It should be illegal."

"Call me criminal then," he whispered and slowly dropped to his knees in front of her. "Are you ready for me?"

"Aren't I always?" she teased, looking down into his eyes.

Yes, he thought, his body leaping into life, his heartbeat hammering in his chest. It was a little game they'd been playing over the last week. No matter what clothes she happened to be wearing when he came home, she made sure she wasn't wearing underwear. After he'd torn through three of her favorite lacy thongs, they'd both decided it would be cheaper—and faster—for her to go without.

All the way home, he'd been imagining this. Thinking about it until he'd nearly driven himself off the road. When had she become so important to him? When had she become the center of his thoughts, the image of his fantasies? And what did it matter now that they were here, together?

"Dev…what're you going to—"

Her words trailed off as he showed her exactly what he'd been thinking about for the last half hour. Thankfully, she was wearing a soft, cotton skirt, which made this all the more easy. Kneeling in front of her, he lifted the flimsy material, dragged it up her thighs and leaned in close enough to taste her.

"Oh! My! Devlin…"

His tongue and lips teased her core. Flicked wildly over the sensitive bud at the heart of her passion and drove them both a little crazed. Her scent, her taste, inflamed him, made him crave more and more of her. Her gasping breaths, her fingers threading through his hair, holding him to her only made him more desperate to push her screaming over the edge.

She twisted against the cooking island, holding on with one hand as she used her free hand to hold his head to her. He glanced up and saw her watching him taste her and that only fed the fires clamoring within. Again and again, he licked and caressed and nibbled. He pushed her higher, faster than he ever had before and could hardly catch his own breath by the time she shrieked his name, trembled violently in his grasp and then slumped bonelessly against him.

"That was—oh my—Devlin, you—" She couldn't even complete a sentence. And he wasn't finished. Not by a long shot. There was more to this fantasy and he wanted it fulfilled now.

Rising, he grabbed her close, kissed her mindless, then lifted her, swung her around and planted her behind down onto the cold, granite counter. She yelped a little, but an instant later, she was lost in their kiss, just as he wanted her.

She was more and more to him every day. Every time he lost himself in her, it only made him want her again. There was no end to this clawing, burning passion. There was only *again*. Fires burned brighter, heat was more explosive and desire fed the need inside him until Devlin could think of nothing but her. How had this happened? How had she slipped so far into his heart, his soul? And how would he ever be able to keep her at a safe distance when everything in him clamored for him to draw her in closer?

She looked at him then and her twilight eyes were dazed with satisfaction and tinged with renewed hunger. She was amazing. She was incredible. And she was his. For now, she was his.

"Devlin," she said on a whisper, "I want you inside me, right this minute."

"That's the plan," he muttered. He opened his zipper, freed himself and moved in close enough to take her there, in their favorite room. He entered her with one long, hard thrust and she gasped at the invasion.

She was tight and hot and welcoming and Devlin let his mind go blank as emotions, *need,* demanded precedence over coherent thought. Rocking his hips, setting a rhythm that she matched eagerly, he pushed them both along that dazzling road to completion until Val groaned, arching into him. Her body flexed, she trembled and in seconds, Dev called out her name and held her tightly as they tumbled into a star-filled chasm.

A few minutes later, Val recovered first, raising her head from his shoulder and smiling at him with so much love it nearly made him breathless. God knew, it made him nervous.

Yes, Dev knew she loved him. She always had. And he…cared for her. God, that was a weak word and he knew it. But he couldn't give her love. Wouldn't allow it of himself. So what he felt for her now, this growing emotion, had to be enough. For both of them.

Disentangling them, Devlin rearranged his clothes,

closed up his zipper, then lifted her off the counter as she smoothed her skirt into place.

"That was quite the greeting," she said, still grinning.

"I like surprises," he told her, already mentally backing away from what he was feeling for her. *Surprises.* Amazing how often that word had come up in the last few weeks. Val's newly discovered self-confidence, the incredible chemistry they shared, his own sense of…affection toward her. He'd been prepared for none of it and that was probably why he was having so damned much trouble dealing with the situation.

Valerie must have picked up on his deepening confusion because her smile faded as she walked back to the cooking island to resume her task.

"Well, I had a surprise today, too."

"Yeah, I was there," he said, leaning back against the counter as he idly considered having the damn thing bronzed.

"Not *that* surprise," she said, tossing him a quick look over her shoulder. "Your mom and I went to a spa today and—"

He came away from the counter, walked to her side and turned her to face him. "You and Mom?"

"Yes," she said, clearly confused by his reaction. "Last weekend at the picnic, we arranged to spend the day together."

He scrubbed one hand across the back of his neck and wondered just how many ways this could be trouble. What had his mother said to her? Had she confessed all her reasons for shattering her family? Did Val sympathize? "That's the surprise?"

"No," Val said, clearly oblivious to his racing

thoughts. "Actually, we had a great time. We had a chance to talk and she…told me about what happened."

Everything in Devlin went from warm to cold in an instant. He stiffened and he felt himself pulling away from her. So Sabrina had talked to her about everything.

"I could tell you—"

"No, thanks." He cut her off fast. He didn't want to hear his mother's secondhand confession. There couldn't be an explanation and an apology was about twenty-five years too late. What was done was done and nothing could be changed.

"Dev, if you'd just let her talk to you—"

He waved one hand and scowled at her. "Never mind about that. What's the surprise you were talking about?"

She sighed, clearly disappointed, but set the knife down, turned to face him and forced a smile. "Well, we were nearly finished at the spa and then we heard these two women—cats, really. They were saying the most horrible things about your mom and about you and me."

Dev gritted his teeth and waited her out. Gossip was nothing new to this town, but the idea of Val and his mother being subjected to actually overhearing the talk about them didn't set well with him. The fact that he was feeling defensive on their behalf didn't really occur to him.

Val kept talking and the more she said, the more Dev's head pounded. This was more than mere gossip. Didn't she see what she'd done? Didn't she get it?

"Anyway," she was saying, "after I finished telling them off, those two took off so fast, I swear you could see sparks flying up from their oh-so-trendy sandals. I was so proud of myself for setting them straight, your mom and I went out to lunch to celebrate."

He stared at her as if he'd never seen her before. "*Celebrate?* Are you nuts?"

"Dev—"

"Damn it, Val, don't you see you've only made this *worse?*"

Ten

Sabrina opened the front door of the Hudson family mansion, stepped inside and paused on the threshold as if she half expected the butler or Hannah, the housekeeper, to come rushing at her to toss her out. But that wouldn't happen. Markus hadn't asked her to leave. She'd gone of her own free will, knowing they both had needed time to deal with the exposure of such a hurtful secret.

But watching Val facing down those malicious gossips at the spa that afternoon had given Sabrina the nudge of courage she'd needed to do a little confronting of her own. She couldn't remain at a hotel for the rest of her life. Not while her heart lived here. In this place. With Markus.

Whether or not it was the right thing to do, she'd had to come home. Had to find out if she still had a marriage to fight for.

Quietly, she moved into the house and, just as quietly, closed the door behind her. She took a long breath to steady herself, then turned around to face the familiar home she'd missed so much. It was so silent, she thought. In the early years, she'd have given any amount of money to find some peace and quiet for an hour or two.

Now, what she wouldn't give to hear her children running through this place. To hear the sounds of their laughter and shouts. To be back in the body of that young wife she'd once been, with the knowledge she now had. But even as she considered that, she knew she couldn't really have changed how her past had played out. Because to do that, she'd have to give up her daughter. And that she couldn't do. Especially now that it looked as though she and Bella were going to be all right.

She'd spoken to Bella on the phone just an hour ago and though the bond between them was fragile, Sabrina knew that the love between them was strong enough to conquer even mortal failings.

After talking with Bella, though, Sabrina had known that she'd have to come here, to this place, to resolve everything else in her life. She'd loved in this house. Raised her children here. This house was as much a part of her as her arms, her legs.

But the man who lived here meant more. So much more.

"God, I was such an idiot," she whispered to no one, her words a hush of sound in the silence.

"No."

She jumped, startled to find she wasn't alone. Markus stepped out of the formal living room to her left and stopped in a slash of lamplight. His features looked strained, but his eyes—the eyes she knew so well—were filled with regret. And seeing that emotion on her husband's face tore at Sabrina with such force, a silent sob wracked her.

And she'd convinced herself she was ready to see him. But how could she? Knowing how hurt he must be? Knowing that her betrayal had cost them both so much?

Covering her mouth with her hand, she turned blindly for the doorknob again. Barely able to speak, she muttered, "I'm sorry, Markus. I shouldn't have come."

He stopped her, laying one hand on her arm. "No, you should never have left."

Slowly, Sabrina raised her gaze to his. "What?"

He smiled. The man she still loved so fiercely, smiled at her and Sabrina's heart settled into a hopeful beat. "I'm so sorry, Sabrina," he said.

Stunned by the one thing she'd never expected to hear from him, she whispered, "Markus, no. I'm the one who should apologize. I never meant to hurt you. Never meant to—"

He took hold of her shoulders, his hands bleeding a welcome warmth into her body after weeks of feeling a bone-deep cold. Sabrina's eyes filled with tears she didn't dare shed for fear of not being able to stop them.

"You don't owe me an explanation, Sabrina," Markus told her and leaned in to kiss her forehead. "I remember what I was like back then. I remember how often I left you alone. How determined I was to keep you at a distance."

True, she thought, all of it true. And why she'd

turned to another man for the attention she'd wanted from her husband.

"Why?" she asked, finally asking the question she should have asked so long ago. "I know you loved me, so why would you want to keep me at bay?"

"*Because* I loved you," he confessed, with a wry smile. "I thought I loved you too much. Thought that if I told you how much I needed you, you would have all the power in our relationship."

"Oh, Markus...."

"I was the fool," he said and shifted one hand to tip her chin up so that he could look directly into her eyes. "I felt you slipping away and did nothing to stop it. I saw David maneuvering you and convinced myself that nothing would happen. I felt your heartache and ignored it."

A single tear traced its way down her cheek and Sabrina didn't bother to wipe it away. Markus did, though. His thumb caught that one stray drop of moisture and his gaze dropped to it. "I didn't mean to hurt you, either, Sabrina," he whispered.

Her heart cracked a little and the pain she'd been clinging to for so long began to seep out and dissolve. Being here with him where she belonged felt so right. How could she ever have risked losing this? Losing him?

Hope filled her, hope that she might regain what she'd lost through selfishness and shortsightedness. But before anything else was said, she had to know something. "Bella. Did you suspect back then that David was her biological father?"

Pain flashed briefly across his features, then was gone an instant later. "Yes," he said softly. "I knew. But it didn't matter. Bella's *mine*. She's *ours*. She always has been."

Her secret, guarded so carefully over the years, had never really been a secret. Ironic? Or was it justice? That she suffered alone and so had Markus, each of them blaming themselves for what had happened and neither of them willing to risk a confession.

"Oh, Markus, I do love you. I've always loved you." She finally raised one hand to wipe away the other tears now raining down her face. "I only got...lost for a while."

"Getting lost isn't important," he said softly. "It only matters that you find your way home. That we *both* found our way home."

"I've missed you so much," she admitted.

He pulled her in close, wrapping his arms around her, and Sabrina drew her first easy breath in weeks. The scent of him, the warm, solid strength of him, so familiar, so very necessary, let her know that she had, finally, come home. Because as much as she loved this house, this *man* was the only home she'd ever really need.

"Never leave me again, Sabrina," he murmured, kissing the top of her head, holding her even more tightly. "I can't live without you."

"Never," she swore, then raised her head so that she could look into his eyes. Smiling, she promised, "I'll always be with you. Always."

His mouth curved, his eyes warmed and he turned her toward the stairs without releasing her. "Let's go upstairs and I'll show you just how much I missed you."

Leaning her head on her husband's shoulder, Sabrina sighed gratefully and wished for her daughter-in-law the same kind of happiness she herself was feeling.

* * *

"Worse?" Val looked at him as if he was out of his mind and that's exactly how Dev felt. "What do you mean? How does standing up for myself and your mother make anything worse?"

Dev cursed under his breath. Man, things could turn to crap in a heartbeat. A few minutes ago, he'd been buried inside his wife, feeling better than he had all day and now...

"Damn it, Val, of *course* you've made things worse."

He shoved both hands through his hair and stalked around the kitchen. He wanted something to kick, but there was nothing in his way. He'd just have to settle for the urge, he supposed. "What the hell were you thinking?"

She was turning in a circle, following him on his mad pace around the room. Violet eyes wide, hands at her hips, she argued, "I was *thinking* about defending myself. And your mother. Protecting this *family.*"

He snorted an unamused laugh. "Nice job."

"What is wrong with you? It was a situation in a salon with a couple of women nobody cares about."

"Right." He stopped dead, looked at her as if he'd never seen her before and said, "In case no one ever told you, this is Hollywood. Those two women will shoot their mouths off all over town. You think they're going to keep quiet about you using your connections at the studio to see they never get an acting job? There's no such thing as a well-kept secret in this town—" As soon as he said those words, though, he realized that his mother had managed to keep her secrets locked away for thirty years, so he added, "usually."

"Dev, I couldn't just sit there while they insulted your mother."

"You damn well should have," he snapped, already seeing imaginary headlines in the morning papers…Hudson Wife Threatens Actress. Perfect. Just perfect.

"Why?"

"Hell, hasn't there been enough bad press about the family? And when those two spread what you said all over town? How's that going to look? My wife telling actresses she can ruin them in this town? Yeah," he muttered, "thanks very much for your help."

She scowled at him, clearly still not seeing the problem here. "You're making too much of this, for heaven's sake."

"And you should mind your own business."

She looked as if he'd slapped her. Her head jerked back, her eyes went wild and wide and she clenched her jaw so tightly, he wouldn't have been surprised to find out she'd ground her teeth to powder.

Finally, though, she took a breath, and said calmly and quietly, "The Hudson family *is* my business. I'm one of you now, whether you want to admit that to yourself or not."

"What the hell does *that* mean?" he shouted and felt the urge to kick something again.

"If you're going to shout, I'm not going to talk to you."

"The hell you're not," he shouted, "we're in the middle of an argument!"

"No, I'm having an argument," she told him flatly. "You're having a tantrum."

"Tantrum." He threw both hands in the air and looked

toward the ceiling and heaven beyond as if searching for help he knew damned well wasn't coming.

"Fine." His voice was tight, but lower now. "What the hell did you mean when you said whether or not I want to admit that you're part of the damned family?"

She blew out a breath, raised her chin and glared at him. "It means, that as long as we're in bed together, you're happy as a clam to have me around. But the minute the sun comes up, you expect me to disappear."

"That's ridiculous." But her words were far too close to the truth for his comfort.

"Is it?" She walked toward him, mouth tight, eyes flashing fire, and Dev backed up a step. He might be furious but he wasn't an idiot.

"This isn't about us," he countered, despite the fury raging in her eyes. "This is about my family's business being talked about all over town and *you* encouraging these morons by threatening them in public!"

"*Our* family is being attacked, Dev. And I defended *your* mother. Something you haven't been able to bring yourself to do."

"Don't start," he warned.

"I didn't start it," she told him hotly, "*You* did. You blame your mother for what happened twenty-five years ago. Well, she blames herself, too."

"As she should—"

"Not finished," Val snapped. "Did it ever occur to you that it takes *two* people to make a good marriage or a bad one?"

"So this is my father's fault?" He shook his head and laughed in her face. "That's great. Perfect. Is that what

Mom told you? That she was *forced* to sleep with my uncle because my father wanted her to?"

"Now you're just being stupid," she said and turned away. "Obviously, you don't want to hear what I'm saying."

He grabbed her forearm, though, and spun her back around to look at him again. "No, finish this. You want it out. Fine. Let's talk about it. My mother betrayed my father. Betrayed *all* of us."

Valerie sighed. "Don't you think she knows that? Don't you think she's sorry?"

"Does being sorry change a damn thing?" he demanded and released her because he felt the need to pace again. To move. So much energy and anger was pumping through him, Dev couldn't have stood still if it meant his life.

"If she changed things, you wouldn't have Bella," Valerie reminded him softly.

He stopped, turned and glared at her. "A low blow."

"Just the truth, Dev," Valerie said and gave another sigh. "I'm not saying your mom didn't make a mistake. What I am saying is that she didn't make that mistake alone. Have you ever considered that maybe if your father hadn't been too busy with his work to even notice he *had* a wife, that none of this might have happened?"

He scowled at her, wanting to push her argument aside, but hadn't he just been thinking something along those lines a few days ago? At the picnic at Jack's house? He'd remembered then how rarely he'd seen his father when he was a kid. Looking back now, with the perspective of an adult, he could see that his mother had been alone most of the time. But even as he admitted that, he heard himself say, "That doesn't give her an excuse to do what she did."

"No, it's not an excuse, but it's a reason," Val said, not letting up on this at all. "Maybe Sabrina needed to feel needed. Needed to know she was loved."

"And sleeping with her brother-in-law did that for her?" He smirked at her. "Nice."

"No, you big jerk, what David did was humiliate her. Use her."

He stared at her, disbelieving. "What?"

"You heard me," Val said and walked toward him again, her eyes still glinting dangerously. "Sabrina was taken advantage of. Her own husband ignored her and the man who seduced her into an affair was really only using her to hurt her husband. So just who was the really injured party here?"

Val's words slapped at him, forced him to realize a few things he'd rather have ignored. For instance, that his mother had feelings in this, too. That maybe his parents' "perfect" marriage had had trouble long before his mother's affair. But he didn't want to acknowledge Val's point, because if he did, he'd have to admit that both his parents were fallible. Not something easily done.

"Don't you see, Dev? There're two sides to every marriage. And if only one person loves, it's doomed to disaster."

He looked into her eyes and realized she was talking about more than his parents' marriage, now. She was talking about them. But they weren't his parents. They understood each other. They had a great sex life. They laughed together. And for God's sake, he damn near raced home every night.

"Our situation is different."

"Is it?"

Irritated beyond measure now, he asked, "It is unless *you're* sleeping with my uncle."

"That's not funny."

"Neither is any of this," he muttered, shoving one hand through his hair as if he could massage away the headache bursting into life behind his eyes.

He looked at Val and tried to find the distance he needed from her. God, he needed it more tonight than ever before. But his own heart was working against him. She was getting to him, reaching some part of him that had been closed off for years.

And the hell of it was, a part of him welcomed it. Thankfully, though, his mind was still in control. Even if everything she'd said about his parents was true, it didn't change the fact that betrayal had torn them apart. His father had trusted his wife and she'd broken faith with him.

How the hell was a man supposed to live with that?

"Dev—"

"Just let it go, Val, okay? For tonight, just let it go." Then he walked past her, needing the outside air, needing to move, to think, away from those violet eyes that saw too much.

"Where are you going?" she called after him.

"Just out back. I need a walk. Clear my head." Then he left, striding into the lamp-lit darkness of the estate.

He stalked to the edge of the garden and looked back at the house where he'd grown up. The argument with Val still buzzing in his brain, Dev let his gaze drift over the old house, until he spotted something at his father's suite. Shadows moving in the lamplight.

Two silhouettes moving toward each other in silence.

He had no trouble recognizing the people—his parents. Clearly, Markus and Sabrina were working out their problems. Shock registered first, then surprise. But then, he thought in disgust, there were plenty of surprises lately in that house.

Turning away, Dev stared out into the night and listened with half an ear to the sounds of the neighborhood. From the end of the street, a yapping dog made itself heard and a car with a powerful engine growled off toward the city.

How in the hell could he not forgive his mother when his father obviously had? And how could he convince himself to forget betrayal and bring himself to trust *anyone* with the power to destroy him?

Disgusted with his parents, his wife and mostly himself, Dev headed off down the greenbelt stretching along the length of the mansions crowding the street.

Looked like he needed that walk more than he'd thought he did.

A few days later, nothing had been settled between Dev and Val, but other problems in the Hudson family were smoothing themselves out.

Val smiled as she walked down the curved staircase toward the family part of the mansion. Sabrina was practically glowing, now that she and Markus had resolved their differences and she had moved back home permanently.

Sabrina had even reconnected with her daughter, though things were still a little fragile at the moment. But Bella was on her way over right now to join Val and

Sabrina for tea and to talk about the upcoming wedding. It seemed that Bella had changed her mind about a quick, uncomplicated ceremony now that she and her mom were speaking again. So the plans would probably take on the scope of the war room at the Defense Department.

Which was good, Val told herself. Anything was good if it kept her mind off her own troubles with Dev. Since their fight in the kitchen the other night, the temperature between them had been cool at best. Yes, their lovemaking retained all the heat and combustion it had before—because neither of them was willing to give up that part of their relationship—but the distance between them otherwise was beginning to broaden.

It was as if even knowing that his parents had made up their differences, Dev was still determined to keep himself locked behind the walls Val had almost given up on smashing.

She stepped onto the marble entryway and turned toward the kitchen and family room. When the phone rang, though, she automatically stepped up to answer it.

"Hello."

"Hi!" A woman's voice, a little hesitant. "Um, who's this?"

Val almost smiled. She recognized the voice easily enough. "Hello, Charlotte, it's Val."

"Val, hi!" The other woman's voice was high, excited and loud enough that she probably could have been heard from her home in France even without the telephone connection.

"I was calling to talk to Aunt Sabrina," she said quickly. "I called the hotel, but they said she'd checked out, so I was sort of hoping she'd gone home and everything was okay now and—"

Now Val did laugh a little. In spite of her own miseries, it was nice to hear someone else so happy. "You were right," she said, interrupting Dev's cousin, "Sabrina did move home a few days ago. I'll go get her for you."

"That'd be great, but wait a sec. I swear I just can't stand not telling somebody, Val, so you get to hear first, just don't tell Aunt Sabrina until I do, okay, because I really want to surprise her and—"

"I promise," Val said, lifting her head as the sound of heels on marble reached her. She smiled at Sabrina as the older woman approached and said, "She's right here, Charlotte—"

"I'm so excited about the baby!" Charlotte gave a delighted laugh.

Val's heart twisted and a pang of envy rattled around inside her even while Charlotte kept talking.

"Honestly, Val, everything is so good here. I never thought I could be this happy, it's just so wonderful…."

"That is great," Val managed to say as Sabrina came up to her, a worried look in her eye.

"And I didn't tell you the best part," Charlotte said quickly, as if sensing that Val was getting ready to hand off the phone. "The baby's a *girl,* and we're going to name her Lillian, after my grandmother."

Another sharp pang jolted Val, despite her best efforts. Family. Connections. Traditions. The Hudsons were moving on, building lives, rebuilding them when necessary and she and Dev were stuck in neutral.

With the frothy sound of Charlotte's happiness ringing

in her ears, and the concerned look on Sabrina's face directly in front of her, Valerie had to acknowledge that she'd made a huge mistake in coming back to Dev. She'd thought she could win his love, but it was obvious to her now that he wasn't interested in what she could give him.

He didn't want to love or be loved. He wanted to be alone while having a sexual partner handy should he require her.

Misery rose up to tangle at the back of her throat and nearly choke her. But somehow, Val managed to say, "Look, Charlotte, your aunt's here, so why don't you tell Sabrina the news about the baby? I've um, got something, to um…"

"Sure, sure. That'd be great. Thanks for listening, Val, and give your husband a big kiss from me!"

"I will. Hold on." Val took the phone from her ear and held it out to Sabrina.

The older woman took it, covered the mouthpiece with her hand and said softly, "Val? Is everything all right?"

"Fine," she said and forced a smile that must have looked as hideous as it felt. "But I don't think I can join you and Bella after all, Sabrina. I've got a few things to take care of today and—"

"It's okay, sweetie," Sabrina said, reaching out to stroke one hand up and down Val's arm in comfort. "But if you need to talk…"

"Thanks," she whispered, already turning back to the stairs. If she didn't leave quickly, the tears building up inside would explode and rain down all over everyone. "I'll see you later, Sabrina."

She couldn't talk to her mother-in-law. Couldn't talk

to anyone about this. The sorrow was just too deep. Too overwhelming. She couldn't live her life watching the people around her grow and be happy and have all the things she wanted so badly for herself. If that made her selfish, then she'd just have to live with it.

Her heels clattered on the marble steps and when she closed herself off in their suite, Val finally gave in to the tears and let them fall, knowing there was no one there to notice.

The moment Dev got home, he instantly knew something was wrong.

No music played.

No tantalizing scents drifted in the air.

Frowning, he walked into the main room, and spotted Val, curled up on a chair by the window, staring out at the garden. She looked beautiful and somehow haunted. "Val?"

She turned her head to look at him and he realized she'd been crying. "What is it? What's wrong?"

"Us," she said softly. "We're what's wrong. Or maybe it's just me. I'm not really sure."

Something cold settled in the middle of his chest as he walked toward her. Sure, things had been a little strained since their last argument, but he'd thought they'd put it behind them. After all, his parents had worked their problems out and he'd even spoken to his mother that morning. So what the hell was wrong now?

"What're you trying to say?" he asked, taking a seat in the chair opposite her.

"I'm saying I want a divorce."

Eleven

Shocked, Dev just stared at her. This he hadn't been expecting. "Where the hell did that come from?"

"Don't sound so stunned," she told him wryly. "Dev, you know this isn't working. We're not happy."

"*I'm* happy and I thought you were, too," he countered, his temper starting to edge past the cold knot of tension in his chest. He was blindsided and trying to make sense of what he was hearing.

"I tried to be." She wrapped her arms around her knees as if for comfort and said, "I really tried this time, Dev. I did. But I'm obviously not the woman you want. You see, I *love* you. I thought I could make you love me, too. But clearly I can't. And since I can't settle for less than love, I can't stay."

"But we're getting along great," he pointed out,

jumping to his feet. "Our sex life is perfect, the family's troubles are winding down, hell, I even talked to Mom this morning because I knew you'd want me to."

She smiled sadly and that tiny expression was enough to shake him to the bone. "I'm glad you're talking to your mom, but don't you see? This isn't about the family. It's about us. And what we don't have. Your cousin Charlotte called to talk about the baby."

"What?"

"Charlotte. She called today from France. The baby's a girl they're naming Lillian."

"Good for her," Dev said, "but what's—"

"She's building a family." She sniffled, wiped her eyes and firmed her mouth. "Jack and Cece have moved on. Max and Dana are engaged. Bella's planning her wedding. Luc and Gwen are nestled in at their ranch. Everyone but *us* is having the kind of life I want. The kind of family I want. The kind we can never have."

"Of course we can."

She shook her head slowly, sadly. "Not without love on both sides, Dev."

"Love?" He snorted the word, shook his head and took two fast steps away from her only to spin around and come right back. "This is about love? Love is over-rated, Val. Look what happened to my parents. *Love* nearly did them in. Their supposedly rock-solid marriage nearly shattered because it was based on love. Is that what you want? Isn't it better to have a relation-ship based on friendship and honest lust?"

She unfolded herself from the chair and stood up to face him. Her mouth trembled but she made a deliberate effort to firm it up. "But it's not just lust on my side, Dev. I love you. And as for your parents' marriage…don't you get it? It's because they love each other that it's going to work out. Love makes every high higher and every low lower. It's what makes life worth living."

"You're wrong," he muttered. "Love's dangerous. Not to be trusted."

"And as long as you feel that way, we won't have anything real." She sighed and crossed her arms, her hands rubbing up and down her upper arms as if for warmth. "I'll stay with you until after the Oscars, Dev. I know how important it is for you to have the family together for that night. But when it's done, I'm leaving. This time for good."

Fear grabbed the base of his throat and he didn't like the taste of it. She seemed so broken. So…sad. She was going to leave. He was going to lose her. And this time there would be no bringing her back. He sensed it instinctively. This was the end. Permanently.

Isn't it better though, his mind taunted, to lose her now, rather than in thirty years? She would have left you eventually. Isn't this way easier?

No. Nothing about this was easy. And no way was he going to let her get away.

"You gave me your word. That day on your patio at your condo…when I went to bring you back home, you swore you wouldn't leave unless I wanted you to," he reminded her. "Well, I don't."

"Yes, you do," she said sadly. "You just don't want to admit it."

"That makes no sense at all."

"None of this does," she agreed. "I'm telling the man

I love that I want a divorce. How is that in any way logical?"

"I'll fight you on the divorce."

"Why?" she asked, one quick flash of hope sparkling in her eyes.

He was breathing heavy, as if he'd run a long race and was only now crossing the finish line, dead last. "Because you're mine. I don't let go of what's mine."

She sighed. "So you don't love me, but you don't want me to leave."

"I *care* about you," Dev said tightly, staring down into twilight eyes glittering with unshed tears. "Can't that be enough?"

"No," she told him. "No, it's not enough. I deserve better. *We* deserve better." Raising one hand, she touched his cheek then reluctantly let her hand fall again. "I'm so sorry, Dev. Sorry for what we could have had. For what we've missed."

When she walked away from him, Dev damn near chased her down. She was making him crazy. Couldn't she see that he was doing this for both their sakes? Love was an unstable emotion. They couldn't risk building a life on something that was so intangible. Couldn't she see that his way was the right way?

He stared after her long after their bedroom door had quietly closed behind her. Emptiness rose up in the shadow-filled room and threatened to swallow him whole. If she left again... No. He wouldn't allow it. Would find a way to stop it. He couldn't lose her. Not now.

He still had some time. She wouldn't leave before the Oscars, so that gave him at least ten or twelve days to change her mind. All he needed were the right words.

Shaking his head, Dev pushed that thought aside as he headed for the door that would take him downstairs into the Hudson family room. What he needed was some of his father's best brandy.

"You look like hell, boy."

Dev stopped in the open doorway of his father's study and looked at the older man seated across the room from him. Markus held an open book in his lap and a tumbler of brandy in his right hand. He could have been an actor on a movie set. The man of leisure at home, surrounded by walls of books, Tiffany-shaded lamps and a crystal carafe of brandy close at hand. Dev had never been more glad to see anyone.

"I've had better days," Dev admitted, then pointed at the brandy. "Got another one of those?"

"Help yourself."

He hadn't counted on seeing his father at the moment, but he realized that this was what he needed. He'd pretty much patterned his life after his father's. Who better to understand the way he felt about his marriage?

Dev poured himself a healthy draught of the French brandy, then took a chair near his father. Staring down into the amber liquid, he searched the surface for the answers to his questions and found nothing.

"So," Markus offered quietly, "you want to talk about whatever's bothering you?"

Snorting a broken laugh, Dev said, "Not really." Then he took a sip of the liquor and felt the fire of it burn right past the knot of cold in his chest. "But I think I need to."

Markus closed the book, set it aside and faced his son. "Shoot."

He should just start talking, Devlin told himself. But where should he start? How to begin?

"You and Mom," he said abruptly. "You've…worked things out?"

Markus frowned a little, took a sip of his own drink and nodded. "We have. I've convinced her to forgive me."

That had Dev's head snapping up and his gaze locking on to his father. "You asked for forgiveness? For *what?*"

"Damn, you really are like me, aren't you?" Markus shook his head and said, "Not everything's black and white, Dev. I made plenty of mistakes early in my marriage. As much as I loved your mother—*do*—love her, I never really allowed her into my heart."

Dev's throat closed up, but he forced another swallow of brandy down anyway.

His father continued, though, as if he hadn't noticed Dev's start of surprise. "I kept a distance between me and your mother. I spent too much time at the studio and not enough with the woman I loved so madly." He chuckled a bit and the sound was soft and sad. "I was so sure I was doing the right thing by holding myself back from her. So positive that was the way to ensure my marriage never overtook my life. Hell, I drove your mother into searching for the affection I denied her."

"She didn't have to betray you," Dev muttered, clutching the brandy snifter as if it were a life raft tossed into a churning sea.

"I betrayed her first," Markus said, leaning forward, bracing his elbows on his knees. "I cut her out of my heart and told myself it was necessary. When the only *really* important thing in the world is love. And the ability to give it as well as receive it."

Dev shook his head. He never would have expected his father to be saying these things and every word the older man said resonated in Dev's heart like a clanging bell echoing over and over again. What the hell was he supposed to think? Do?

"Dev, let me tell you something else," Markus said softly, "when you're an old man, looking back at your life, it'll be nice to remember the awards and things— but if you're looking back alone, it will mean your life was a failure."

Silence dropped over the room until the only sound was Dev's own breathing and the soft muffled tick of the clock on the wall. His mind was racing, his heart was pounding and one thought after another chased themselves through his brain. And every thought had one thing in common. Valerie.

"How? How do you do it?" he asked, slanting a glance at his father. The man he'd loved and admired his entire life. "How do you let yourself trust?"

"You find the right woman, like I did. Like *you* did. Cut yourself a break, son. Open yourself up before you miss everything worthwhile. Don't be the man I was. Be a better man. A wiser man."

Wiser. He'd thought he was wise in keeping himself cut off from his wife. But what kind of wisdom was that when it felt as though he was cutting his own heart out of his chest to be without her?

Markus shifted his gaze to the doorway and smiled broadly. "Sabrina."

Dev shot to his feet, turned around and watched his

mother's hesitation as she looked at him. Was she expecting to be shunned? For him to turn away from her? Well, why the hell wouldn't she? He'd been a roaring jerk for weeks, why would his mother have guessed that he'd finally come to his senses?

Setting his brandy snifter down on the table, he walked across the room, his gaze locked on his mother's. And when he was close enough, he wrapped his arms around her, pulled her in tight and held on as though he were a child again and needed the comfort only she could offer. "Mom, I'm so sorry."

She cried. One short, sharp sob, then she was holding him back, murmuring his name and rubbing her hands up and down his back just the way she used to. "Oh, Dev, honey, me, too."

"I know." He straightened up, smiled at her and said, "I've been a jerk for weeks. Hell, years. But I think I'm finally catching on."

She tilted her head to one side, gave him a knowing smile and asked, "Does Val know about this epiphany?"

"She's about to find out," he told her, already headed for the stairs that led to his suite. "Wish me luck."

"Luck," Sabrina whispered as her husband came up behind her and enfolded her in a tender embrace.

Val couldn't breathe.

She opened the windows in the bedroom she shared with Dev and lifted her face into the wind, and still it didn't help. She couldn't seem to draw air into her lungs and she guessed it was because her heart had shattered in her chest and the airways were blocked.

She couldn't believe it had come to this. She'd had

so much hope, so many plans. And she loved Devlin Hudson so very much. How could it all have dissolved so quickly, so painfully?

"Val!"

"Oh, God…" She swiped her hands under her eyes and steeled herself for whatever argument he might have come up with in the last half hour. But it didn't matter what he said. She couldn't stay with him, loving and never knowing what it felt like to be loved in return.

Val heard him rushing from room to room in the apartment, but didn't say a word, not anxious to once again have her heart stepped on. Finally, though, he came into the room behind her and she was forced to turn and face him.

"I thought you'd left," he said.

"I told you I'd stay until after the Oscars."

"Right. Of course you did. Look, Val…"

She held up one hand. "Please, Dev. If you don't mind, I'd rather not have the same argument again tonight. I'm just too…"

"No argument," he said and walked toward her with several long determined steps. "Just an apology."

She blinked at him, not really sure she'd heard him correctly. "An apology? For what?"

"Being a jerk," he blurted. "Not being what you needed. What we *both* needed."

Valerie felt a little dizzy all of a sudden and was forced to lock her knees in place to keep from falling over. Her heart gave a quick, hard thump in her chest. "What're you saying?"

"I'm saying I love you."

She swayed and he reached out to steady her. His

hands hard and firm on her upper arms, she felt the heat of his touch sliding down inside to ease the pain and erase the emptiness. "You what?"

"Love you. Wildly. Passionately. Desperately. I love the way you think. Your laugh. Your sighs. I love how your eyes look like the sky at twilight just when the stars first come out."

"Dev—" Oh, God, could this be happening? Could she really be hearing what she'd dreamed of hearing from him?

"You're smart, you're funny and you make me think. You make me a better man." He pulled her in closer, stared down into her eyes and smiled as he'd never smiled before. "I thought I could keep you at arm's length. Protect my heart. But you *are* my heart."

"Oh, Devlin, I love you so much."

"Good," he said, grinning now. "That's very good. I want us to go away together," he added. "Now. We'll take that honeymoon we never really had. We'll go to Bali or Europe or…wherever the hell you want to go."

"Now?" she said, laughing, hope rising up inside her like the most brilliant sunrise she could have imagined. "We can't go now, the Oscars."

He cupped her face in his hands and said softly, "Doesn't mean a thing to me. Screw Hollywood. All I need is you."

It was like waking up on Christmas morning and finding just what you'd wished for waiting for you. Val threw her arms around his neck and held on for all she was worth. "You don't know how much I love hearing you say that."

"I mean it, Val. All of it."

"I know you do. And not that I'm not enjoying this, but what happened? What's changed?"

"Me. I've changed. Being with you, loving you has changed me completely. I just didn't want to admit it. But those days are over."

"I can see that," she whispered, "and I'll take you up on your honeymoon offer the minute the Oscars are over."

"Deal," he said quickly. "And there's something else, too. We're moving out of the manor."

"What?" She drew her head back to look up into the eyes she loved so much.

"We're going to get our own place. Anywhere you want." He paused, then said, "Hey, the place two doors down from Jack's in Malibu was for sale. How about that?"

"The beach?" Her heart was racing, her skin was humming and her mind was filled with so much happiness, she didn't think she could take much more. She remembered the house he was talking about. Very Cape Cod. Very homey. Very perfect. "That would be wonderful."

"Done," he announced. "We'll buy it tomorrow. You can redecorate it every week, so I can break my legs on tables that shouldn't be there."

Valerie laughed giddily.

"And it has to have a great kitchen," he added, kissing her quickly, once, twice.

"With granite counters," she suggested.

"Oh, definitely," Dev agreed. "You'll see, Val. We'll build our own family. Our own place. Our own memories and traditions."

"With love," she promised.

"With more love than I ever thought possible," he

admitted, sounding like a man who'd finally found the road home.

"Oh, Devlin," Val whispered, looking up at him with stars in her eyes and love swamping her heart. The man she loved, loved her back and that was all she'd ever really needed. "Stop talking now and kiss me."

"Your wish," he said with a grin, "is my command."

Epilogue

The Hudson table at the after-Oscar party was loud and celebrational. *Honor* had not only taken Best Picture of the year, but awards for Best Director, Best Actress, set design, and so many others, Dev could hardly keep them all straight.

And it didn't matter anyway.

Dev had already won the most important thing in his life. The Oscars were just the frosting on the cake.

"To the Hudsons," he proposed, lifting his champagne glass and looking around the table at the family gathered there. His parents, his brothers and sister, his cousins and most especially, his beautiful wife. "We did it. We honored Charles and Lillian. We made the world see them as we knew them. And we did it with a hell of a lot of style."

Lots of applause, cheers and laughter followed that statement.

But Dev wasn't finished. "It's been a full year. For all of us." His gaze shifted from one familiar face to the next and love for his family overwhelmed him.

Val had given him this, he told himself and counted his blessings again. She'd opened him up to the possibilities surrounding him and he'd never again be the closed-off man he was when he'd first met her.

He sent a silent thanks to the fates that had guided him to her and he'd never stop being grateful to her for not giving up on him.

But his family was watching him, waiting.

So he smiled, reached down for Val's hand and closed his fingers around hers. Still holding his glass high, he ignored the roar of noise from the surrounding partiers and the music blasting down from the overhead speakers.

"We came through. All of us. The Hudsons are a family and that's where our strength comes from. It's what we draw on, what we lean on, what we depend on."

Smiles and nods greeted him and he felt like a damn king as he added, "To the family. To the heart of us. And next year…we win it *all*."

While their table erupted in cheers and laughter and kisses, Dev sat down, looked at Val and smiled. "I love you."

She grinned back at him, leaned in and kissed him hard and long, silently promising all sorts of private celebrations when they got home. "I'll never get tired of hearing that, you know."

"Thank God," he said softly.

Then as his parents left the table to dance, Val leaned in close again and whispered in his ear, "Are you up for another surprise?"

"With you? Always."

"I think I'm pregnant."

He jerked back, looked at her in stunned surprise and then laughed, loud and long. Standing up, he dragged her to her feet, then wrapped his arms around her and swung her in a tight circle. She held on tight and her laughter sounded like music to him.

"Make me a promise," he whispered.

"Anything."

"Never stop surprising me."

* * * * *

ALEXANDROS KAREDES, SNOW DUSTING the shoulders of his leather jacket and glittering like jewels in his dark hair, stood at the door. Maria felt the blood drain from her head.

"Good evening, Ms. Santos."

His voice was as she remembered it. Deep. Husky. Perfect English, but with the faintest hint of a Greek accent. And cold, as cold as it had been that awful morning she would never forget, when he'd accused her of horrible things, called her terrible names….

"Aren't you going to ask me in?"

She fought for composure. Last time they'd faced each other, they'd been on his turf. Now they were on hers. She was in command here, and that meant everything.

"There's a sign on the door downstairs," she said, her tone every bit as frigid as his. "It says, 'No soliciting or vagrants.'"

His lips drew back in a wolfish grin. "Very amusing."

"What do you want, Prince Alexandros?"

A tight smile eased across his mouth and it killed her that even now, knowing he was a vicious, arrogant man, she couldn't help but notice what a handsome mouth it was. Chiseled. Generous. Beautiful, like the rest of him, which made him living proof that beauty could, indeed, be only skin deep.

"Such formality, Maria. You were hardly so proper the last time we were together."

She knew his choice of words was deliberate. She felt her face heat; she couldn't help that but she damned well didn't have to let him lure her into a verbal sparring match.

"I'll ask you once more, your highness. What do you want?"

"Ask me in and I'll tell you."

"I have no intention of asking you in. Tell me why you're here or don't. It's your choice, just as it will be my choice to shut the door in your face."

He laughed. It infuriated her but she could hardly blame him. He was tall—six two, six three—and though he stood with one shoulder leaning against the door frame, hands tucked casually into the pockets of the jacket, his pose was deceptive. He was strong, with the leanly muscled body of a well-trained athlete.

She remembered his body with painful clarity. The feel of him under her hands. The power of him moving over her. The taste of him on her tongue.

Suddenly, he straightened, his laughter gone. "I have not come this distance to stand in your doorway," he said coldly, "and I am not going to leave until I am ready to do so. I suggest you stand aside and stop behaving like a petulant child."

A petulant child? Was that what he thought? This man who had spent hours making love to her and had then accused her of—of trading her body for profit?

Except it had not been love, it had been sex. And the sooner she got rid of him, the better.

She let go of the doorknob and stepped aside. "You have five minutes."

He strolled past her, bringing cold air and the scent of the night with him. She swung toward him, arms folded. He reached past her, pushed the door closed, then folded his arms, too. She wanted to open the door again but she'd be damned if she was going to get into a who's-in-charge-here argument with him. She was in charge, and he would surely see a tussle over the ground rules as a sign of weakness.

Instead, she looked past him at the big clock above her work table.

"Ten seconds gone," she said briskly. "You're wasting time, your highness."

"What I have to say will take longer than five minutes."

"Then you'll just have to learn to economize. More than five minutes, I'll call the police."

Instantly, his hand was wrapped around her wrist. He tugged her toward him, his dark-chocolate eyes almost black with anger.

"You do that and I'll tell every tabloid shark I can contact about how Maria Santos tried to buy a five-hundred-thousand-dollar commission by seducing a prince." He smiled thinly. "They'll lap it up."

* * * * *

*What will it take for this
billionaire prince to realize he's
falling in love with his mistress…?
Look for*
BILLIONAIRE PRINCE, PREGNANT MISTRESS
*by Sandra Marton
Available July 2009
from Harlequin Presents®.*

We'll be spotlighting a different series every month throughout 2009 to celebrate our 60th anniversary.

Look for Harlequin® Presents in July!

TWO CROWNS, TWO ISLANDS, ONE LEGACY
A royal family, torn apart by pride and its lust for power, reunited by purity and passion

Step into the world of Karedes beginning this July with

BILLIONAIRE PRINCE, PREGNANT MISTRESS
by
Sandra Marton

Eight volumes to collect and treasure!

THE BELLES OF TEXAS

They're as strong as the state that raised
them. The Belle sisters aren't afraid to go
after what they want, whether it's reclaiming
their ranch or their family.

Linda Warren
CAITLYN'S PRIZE

Thanks to her deceased father's gambling
debts, Caitlyn Belle's beloved High Five Ranch
is in dire straits. Particularly because the
will stipulates that if the ranch doesn't turn
a profit in six months, it must be sold to
Judd Calhoun—the man Caitlyn jilted
fourteen years ago. And Cait knows Judd has
been waiting a long time for his revenge....

*Look for the first book
in The Belles of Texas miniseries,
on sale in July wherever books are sold.*

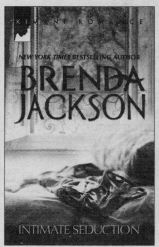

REQUEST YOUR FREE BOOKS!

2 FREE NOVELS PLUS 2 FREE GIFTS!

▼ Silhouette®

Desire®

Passionate, Powerful, Provocative!

YES! Please send me 2 FREE Silhouette Desire® novels and my 2 FREE gifts (gifts are worth about $10). After receiving them, if I don't wish to receive any more books, I can return the shipping statement marked "cancel". If I don't cancel, I will receive 6 brand-new novels every month and be billed just $4.05 per book in the U.S. or $4.74 per book in Canada. That's a savings of almost 15% off the cover price! It's quite a bargain! Shipping and handling is just 50¢ per book.* I understand that accepting the 2 free books and gifts places me under no obligation to buy anything. I can always return a shipment and cancel at any time. Even if I never buy another book, the two free books and gifts are mine to keep forever.

225 SDN EYMS 326 SDN EYM4

Name	(PLEASE PRINT)	
Address		Apt. #
City	State/Prov.	Zip/Postal Code

Signature (if under 18, a parent or guardian must sign)

Mail to the Silhouette Reader Service:
IN U.S.A.: P.O. Box 1867, Buffalo, NY 14240-1867
IN CANADA: P.O. Box 609, Fort Erie, Ontario L2A 5X3

Not valid to current subscribers of Silhouette Desire books.

**Want to try two free books from another line?
Call 1-800-873-8635 or visit www.morefreebooks.com.**

* Terms and prices subject to change without notice. Prices do not include applicable taxes. Sales tax applicable in N.Y. Canadian residents will be charged applicable provincial taxes and GST. Offer not valid in Quebec. This offer is limited to one order per household. All orders subject to approval. Credit or debit balances in a customer's account(s) may be offset by any other outstanding balance owed by or to the customer. Please allow 4 to 6 weeks for delivery. Offer available while quantities last.

Your Privacy: Silhouette Books is committed to protecting your privacy. Our Privacy Policy is available online at www.eHarlequin.com or upon request from the Reader Service. From time to time we make our lists of customers available to reputable third parties who may have a product or service of interest to you. If you would prefer we not share your name and address, please check here. ☐

SDES09R

In 2009 Harlequin celebrates
60 years of pure reading pleasure!

We're marking this occasion by offering
16 **FREE** full books to download and read.

Visit

www.HarlequinCelebrates.com

to choose from a variety of
great romance stories
that are absolutely **FREE!**

(Total approximate retail value of $60)

We invite you to visit and share the Web site
with your friends, family
and anyone who enjoys reading.

Silhouette Desire

COMING NEXT MONTH
Available July 14, 2009

#1951 ROYAL SEDUCER—Michelle Celmer
Man of the Month
The prince thought his bride-to-be knew their marriage was only a diplomatic arrangement. But their passion in the bedroom tells a different story....

**#1952 TAMING THE TEXAS TYCOON—
Katherine Garbera**
Texas Cattleman's Club: Maverick County Millionaires
Seducing his secretary wasn't part of the plan—yet now he'll never be satisfied with just one night.

#1953 INHERITED: ONE CHILD—Day Leclaire
Billionaires and Babies
Forced to marry to keep his niece, this billionaire finds the perfect solution in his very attractive nanny...until a secret she's harboring threatens to destroy everything.

#1954 THE ILLEGITIMATE KING—Olivia Gates
The Castaldini Crown
This potential heir will only take the crown on one condition—he'll take the king's daughter with it!

**#1955 MAGNATE'S MAKE-BELIEVE MISTRESS—
Bronwyn Jameson**
Secretly determined to expose his housekeeper's lies, he makes her his mistress to keep her close. But little does he know that he has the wrong sister!

**#1956 HAVING THE BILLIONAIRE'S BABY—
Sandra Hyatt**
After one hot night with his sister's enemy, he's stunned when she reveals she's carrying his baby!

SDCNMBPA0609